PIRATES WANTED

FOR A HAZARDOUS VOYAGE. LOW RATIONS. MERCILESS STORMS. LONELY WATCHES IN FOG-BOUND WATERS. CONSTANT ATTACKS AND LOSS OF CREW. FOR THOSE WHO ENDURE: UNSHAKEABLE PEACE. INCORRUPTIBLE TREASURE. AND A SEAT AT THE GOOD CAPTAIN'S TABLE.

A ship's crew who can't hear the commands of their captain is destined to drift off course and end up smashed among the rocks. Two-way dialogue between the captain and the hands on deck is a nonnegotiable for any healthy crew. The sad truth is that countless people are not on speaking terms with God, have never heard His voice, and pray only monologue requests. Many are closer to the brink of shipwreck with God than they know. I wrote this book for pirates starving to find greater treasure that changes everything: abundant life as best friends with God and His people, no strings attached. And to have fun doing it.

WARNING: This book's structure is innovative, but nothing you can't handle. I believe you'll enjoy the new rhythm once you settle into it. Within its pages, two stories sail side by side. The top paragraph, ***written in italics***, is a continuous fictional pirate tale. The paragraph beneath is my real spiritual journey, explaining the meaning behind each parable. Both stories can stand on their own, but when read together, they reveal deeper treasure. I promise to share these experiences honestly, without embellishment. They may sound otherworldly, but they're true. Just ask my mates. I'm no more special than you; the same treasure is yours to find. The Good Captain looks across every shore for sailors who dare to seek Him, inviting each one into the voyage of a lifetime. So don't stay landlocked, brave the seas, and go find your treasure!

-Pirate Parker

LEGAL

Published in Nashville, Tennessee, by
WONSER PARK LLC
www.wonserpark.com | info@wonserpark.com

Edited by Cara Lena Marchesani
Graphic Design and Logo by Parker Wonser
Photography by Anna Müller

ISBN: 979-8-218-78274-0
10 9 8 7 6 5 4 3 2 1

Printed in the United States of America

Pirate Property:

____

"Pirate Parables brought me back to the simple joy of wonder, the kind that makes you believe again that God still hides treasures in plain sight for those willing to seek."

-**Dustin Smith**, Lead Pastor of Parker's home church HopeUC Nashville & founder of Here Be Lions

Contents

PIES

Remember the smell of pie baking, filling the house and drawing people into the kitchen without a word being spoken? Like that aroma, parables draw hearts through story, opening doors to deeper truths. Jesus chose this style of teaching, offering simple, relatable images that lingered in the mind and invited reflection. Rather than forcing lessons, He created space for listeners to ponder and discover in their own time. In the same way, these parables are written to spark curiosity and gently invite readers to taste the richness of God's truth.

2 Corinthians 2:14-15

Cōws

Like a cow chewing each blade of grass again and again to draw out every bit of nourishment, these parables are best approached with patience. They are meant to be read slowly and returned to often, allowing new layers of meaning to unfold. What begins as a simple story may become a living connection, something to share with others, a spark of faith, or a reminder of God-given worth.

Psalm 1:2-3

PIRATE

A lost pirate finds great treasure...

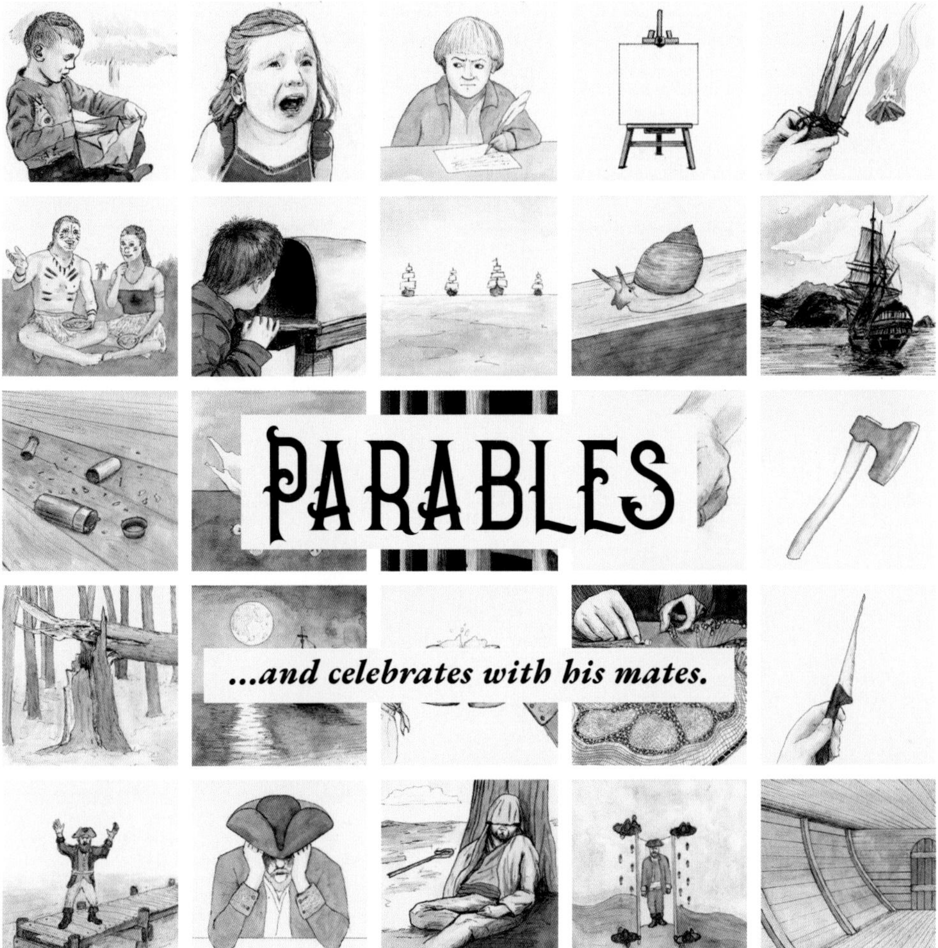
PARABLES
...and celebrates with his mates.

A LŌST PIRATE...

Anything out there?

Psalm 13:1-2

MŌUNTAIN TREASURE

Pirate Parable

In 17th-century Shaftesbury, England, a young boy sat through grammar school lessons with little interest until the other boys whispered of a pirate's hidden treasure. It was said to be a chest too full to be spent in one lifetime, buried where no trail could reach. The legend came in rhyme, passed from boy to boy like contraband:

"A pirate hid his treasure deep,
too much to spend in one life's keep.
It watches where the skies unfold,
through searing sun and winds grown cold.
No soul around, no trail or track,
the chest lies still, the key intact."

Some swore their fathers believed it was hidden atop a snowy mountain in the Alps, where the sun shone bright but the snow erased every footprint. No one knew if it was real, but it was all the boy ever thought about. That treasure became the boy's secret daydream, a sparkling hope buried under the weight of his dull, farm life. He didn't want to tend grain fields.

Parker's Journey

As a child, I felt crushed beneath the weight of religion, where "God" seemed more like a tyrant than a Father. The people around me tried to earn His favor through rigid routines and lifeless habits, leaving me confused. How could the Bible promise freedom when I only felt trapped? I saw Scripture not as a living invitation, but as a closed record of long-gone miracles, as if God had spoken once and never again. It felt like people worshiped the book itself rather than the One it spoke of. Still, now and then, I heard whispers of wild stories, of healing, of encounters, of voices from heaven. I doubted them, yet something stirred. *What if they were true?* That question never left me.

Matthew 13:44

Talking Fish

The Boy lived a hard and lonely life, constantly aching for escape. After being expelled from school, he spent two bitter years laboring on the farm, disappointed and exhausted. His father worked sun-up to sun-down, and his mother dismissed his talk of life beyond the farm with trembling warnings: ***"The world out there is dark... thieves, storms, and sickness wait for fools who wander too far."*** *But the Boy could not shake the feeling that he was made for more. He would often creep to the edge of the fields and watch the moon rise over distant hills, imagining treasure, adventure, and a crew of pirate comrades. One night, in a deep sleep, he had a vivid dream of fish scattered across his family's land, gasping under the sun, their scales cracking in the dry heat. He urged them toward the pond, shouting that they were made to swim, breathe, live. But the fish only scoffed, claiming they were fine and had always lived this way.*

Growing up felt like walking through fog. I was enrolled in a private classical school but struggled to keep up. I could not read well and spent most of my childhood believing I was stupid. It took until 11th grade to realize it was undiagnosed dyslexia that made every assignment feel like a mountain. And in a literature-heavy school, I fell behind constantly, seen as lazy and unfocused. To survive, I sharpened my ears and learned to intuitively feel my way through the world, which helped develop my creativity. During this time, our family moved houses ten times, making lasting friendships nearly impossible. With no brothers, no nearby friends, and a father who traveled for work, I often played Legos alone. In ninth grade, a knee injury ended my soccer life, leaving me further isolated with three years of rehab. Around then, my oldest sister dropped out of school to get treatment for debilitating Obsessive-Compulsive Disorder, and my parents' attention turned to her recovery. I felt invisible, a background character in my own story. The advice I received was, "*You'll be fine, it's normal.*" But that didn't suffice for long.

John 10:10

CLOUDY NIGHT

The disturbing dream lingered in his mind. He saw himself in those gasping fish; told they were fine while slowly dying in a place they were never meant to live. It was a sign. That very night, he crept into his parents' room, stole a pouch of coins, packed a small sack, and slipped away without a sound. For two days, he walked toward Poole Harbor, his heart pounding with fear and fire. He had dreamed of joining a pirate crew for as long as he could remember, and now the wind smelled of salt and freedom. When he finally boarded a merchant ship bound for Port Royal, he felt the world open wide for the first time. That night at sea, overcast clouds swallowed the stars, and he stood at the rail watching the sky disappear. He knew nothing of sailing and wondered how a ship could find its way when the stars were hidden. But the crew showed no signs of doubt. The stars were still there, even if unseen, and somehow, the ship kept moving forward.

The clouds always seemed heavy; I never saw the stars. At my childhood churches, God was spoken of like a myth behind clouds; always present, never seen. Sermons felt hollow, the leaders', spiritually lifeless, and legalism stifled any sense of wonder. If humans had spoken of God for thousands of years, surely someone must have seen something real. Or was faith just a joyless crawl, forcing beliefs down my throat with nothing to nourish the soul? When I asked hard questions, I was silenced or told that God keeps things hidden. The control I saw in church disgusted me. Giving my life to God sounded exhausting; since even offering a part of it felt like too much. Besides, I knew atheists who were happier than any Christian I'd met. At sixteen, I left home to live with my aunt and uncle in Michigan. I was determined to search for what was real. If God wasn't the answer, I would keep asking, keep digging, and let the truth rise, wherever it came from.

Hebrews 11:6

PORT LIZARDS

After seven long weeks at sea, the boy stepped onto the noisy and chaotic docks of Port Royal. The hot air pulsed with shouts and music; the streets teemed with rough men, hands hovering near their weapons. The stench of sweat and rum clung to everything. He recalled the sailors' jokes about Port Lizards and soon learned they were not creatures, but women who sold their company to pirates. These women crowded every tavern. There were no wives or children in sight. Fistfights erupted in the streets over women, cards, and coins. He stepped over unconscious men sprawled out. The city bled pain and pleasure, soaked in liquor and desperation. But there was wealth, more than he'd dreamed. Pirates strutted through the alleys in embroidered coats, jeweled swords at their sides, rings gleaming like royal treasure. Their motto was simple: ***take what you can, and grow rich.*** *He'd fled the farm in search of more. And here it was. If he wanted their luxury, he'd have to learn their ways.*

In high school, I went camping in northern Michigan with my 14-year-old cousin Brock. We slept near a river, tying our backpacks in a tree to keep them from animals. During the night, snapping branches and heavy footsteps woke us. In the moonlight, I saw a massive black bear climbing the tree, swatting at our bags, just 15 feet from my head. I lay frozen on the ground, no tent, as the bear tore into our bags and dragged them around the woods. For two hours, I shook with fear, sure we were next. Even as an atheist, I instinctively prayed for God to save us. When morning came and we were unharmed, I felt deep relief. But what stayed with me wasn't survival; it was the realization that I only called on God when I wanted something. I wanted the fruit of His protection without the roots of a real relationship, if He was even real. That night exposed the emptiness of my own spiritual hookup culture; no different than the pirates who used Port Lizards for fleeting comfort.

Matthew 11:28-29

FEARMŌNGER

To survive among pirates, the Boy quickly learned that cruelty was currency. He grew close to an older helmsman with a peg leg. A man from his own hometown of Shaftesbury, once a sailor in the Royal Navy before defecting. The helmsman was set to sail in a month aboard the **Fearmonger**, *the largest ship in port. They spent many days walking the hills above town, swapping tales of the sea. The man shared stories of narrow escapes, but also warned of the pirate life: scorching heat, endless months at sea, and blood-soaked wages that often never came. But the Boy wouldn't be swayed. On the morning of the ship's departure, as they hiked through the hills, the boy waited until the man turned his back, then struck his good leg with a heavy branch, snapping the bone clean. He ran back to the port as the man's screams faded behind him. There, he posed as the helmsman's nephew, an experienced sailor ready to take his place. It was his first true pirate act, and he felt no shame.*

I figured if God was not going to show up, I would have to find my own way through life. I rejected Him and entered university for industrial design. I began trying to find something that could satisfy my soul. I had been lonely for as long as I could remember, and being socially awkward made it even harder. I thought getting a girlfriend would fix it. I started manipulating girls into relationships, not because I wanted to hurt them, but because I was desperate to feel loved. For a moment, it felt like it worked, but deep down, I knew I was using people, and that it would leave us all wounded. I was not trying to be cruel. I was just surviving the only way I knew how. But as the pattern repeated, I began to believe a deeper lie. Maybe I was simply bad at love. Maybe I would be alone forever.

Romans 7:19

Friendly Forest

When the Boy told the captain of the **Fearmonger** *that he was the peg-legged helmsman's nephew, the captain hesitated. Yet the Boy knew so many details of the man's life that, pressed for time, the captain accepted his story and welcomed him aboard. The boy stood at the stern, marveling at the towering vessel beneath his feet. As Port Royal's jungle-wrapped coastline shrank and forests blurred into green shadows, he was awestruck. This whole ship, he realized, had come from trees that fed the hungry, shaded the weary, warmed the cold, and now carried men across oceans. Even cut down, they served with strength and grace. And yet this mighty ship, born of such generosity, would be used to rob and destroy. Still, the trees had given themselves freely.*

One memory shines as an example of God's radical generosity, like a tree offering provision when I didn't deserve it. After a fiery breakup with a French girl I had been dating abroad, I hit rock bottom and flew back to Michigan. My layover in NYC landed at 3:00 a.m. I was jet-lagged, exhausted, and heartbroken. I slept barely an hour before heading to my gate at 5:00 a.m. Then delays began. One hour stretched into six, and eventually, storms canceled flights across the airport. I ended up in a four-hour line at Spirit Airlines, completely drained. Out of desperation, I prayed despite doubting God's existence. I felt a nudge to talk to a father and son who had just left the counter. They reported the next flight to Michigan wasn't for four days, so they were renting a car to drive home. I couldn't wait four days. Another nudge came: *Ask if you can join their ride*. I did, and they said yes. They turned out to be Christians, and we drove 12 hours through the night, getting me home just in time for classes. I was stunned. After being a scumbag boyfriend in France, God still answered my prayer, generous as a tree, giving shade to someone who hadn't earned it.

Matthew 5:45

BILGE PUMP

*After several days at sea, the crew prepared to raid a nearby island, but a burst of hurricane winds snapped ropes and sent the ship into chaos. When the storm passed, the captain ordered everyone below deck to retrieve spare lines. It was the boy's first time descending to the lowest level, far beneath the helm where he usually stood. The air thickened with mildew and sweat. Puddles covered the floor, and to his surprise, three men were already there, straining at the bilge pump. Their skin glistened, their hands moved with exhausted rhythm. He asked how long they'd been down there. One replied, "**The job never ends.**" Low-ranking crew worked in shifts to keep the leaky ship afloat. Day and night. As he climbed back up with ropes in hand, the Boy's chest tightened with a quiet truth: if he hadn't struck the peg-legged man and lied to the captain, this would have been his place. A dark, damp hell, pouring out water that only leaked back in.*

I started believing that since I was alone, everything depended on me. Success felt like a burden I had to carry solo, so I set out to be the best. In college, I became obsessed with perfection: cutting out bad habits, devouring self-help books, optimizing routines, chasing excellence with ruthless focus. I excelled in industrial design, developing innovative products for companies across a variety of industries, including music technology, furniture, toys, and medical devices. I performed stand-up comedy at local open mics to sharpen my humor and charisma. My life became a nonstop hustle, like a sailor at the bilge pump, frantically scooping water to keep from sinking, trying to stay afloat by removing every trace of weakness. I worked seven days a week, thinking that if I achieved enough, I'd finally feel peace. But the more I scooped, the more emptiness leaked in. Eventually, I crashed; burned out, drained, disoriented. That's when I realized maybe hustling wasn't the way forward. But if not that, then what? How could I get ahead or rise above if I wasn't the best?

Matthew 11:28-30

Hollow Victories

Over months at sea, the crew grew fond of the Boy, admiring his sharp humor, easy charm, and the way he captured each of them in portraits sketched with surprising skill. The captain, in particular, developed a special liking for him. As time passed, the Boy proved himself a tenacious fighter in battle, earning respect and a generous share of the loot. Yet the gold never lasted. Raids became routine, and the danger, violence, and victories turned into a kind of drug. He transformed into a ruthless warrior who spared no lives when attacking ships and towns, finding dark satisfaction in dominating the powerless. Theft turned into cold-blooded murder. His growing brutality impressed the crew, and he joined them in celebrating each raid with increasing abandon, drinking heavily and squandering his wealth on pleasures at port. As the money ran dry, he felt compelled to plan even grander conquests to keep the thrill alive. Outwardly, he appeared to be a happy pirate, but inside, he was falling apart, haunted by the knowledge that this reckless life could not last.

Lonely and exhausted, I began to believe I was powerless and needed something outside myself to find peace. I turned to alcohol, thinking it would help me fit in, but it only deepened the emptiness. The more I drank, the more I needed just to feel normal, and the worse I felt the next day. Then I found marijuana, and for the first time, my anxiety vanished. I slept deeply, and it felt like I had discovered the secret to peace. I thought to myself, *So this is how people live, without constant fear.* But within a month, the high turned on me. My memory faltered. My mind grew foggy and slow, like someone had downgraded the processor in my brain. I forgot names, lost sharpness, and couldn't sleep without getting high. My mental health declined, and the thought of quitting felt terrifying. One night, curled on my bedroom floor feeling completely burnt out, I whispered a question I had never asked before. God… *what if you are real*?

Jeremiah 2:13

BARBACŌA

Back in England, the Boy had heard wild tales from Spanish sailors about a food called **barbacoa**, *said to be the greatest meat ever cooked. Slow-roasted over fire, tender and rich with flavor. He once tried an English imitation and found it so foul he dismissed the legend as nonsense. But months later, when the crew stopped in Puerto Rico, the local tribes prepared something by the same name. When the pirates offered him a serving, he refused, waving it off. The crew mocked him, calling him soft. Still, he held his ground. Eventually, laughing and persistent, they shoved a chunk into his hand and told him to stop acting like a Brit. The moment it touched his tongue, the world stopped. Smoky, juicy, rich beyond imagining. It melted in his mouth and filled his chest with warmth. He nearly wept. No rumor had done it justice. No words could. It was the finest thing he'd ever tasted. He ate until his belly ached, and his doubts were gone.*

In search of fulfillment, I tried everything: high performance, substances, manipulative relationships. But nothing worked. By my senior year of university, I was anxious, depressed, and suicidal. Desperate, I cried out to God: if He could lift the weight of my depression, I'd give Him my life. If not, I planned to end it. As a final escape, I flew to Florida to spend Christmas break with a friend and his six roommates. My plan was to have fun partying, then come home and end it all. But those seven guys were men of peace. For five weeks, I tasted nothing but kindness and unconditional hospitality. They let me use their cars, share their food, and borrow their surfboards. No sermons. No pressure. Just welcome. They were single, financially humble, drug-free, and radiated joy. I learned that they were deeply connected to God, full of freedom and love, and best friends with Jesus. I hated them talking about God... but I loved their lives. And I wondered: what was stopping me from finding that kind of freedom?

Psalm 34:8

CARDS

During the last victorious raid, the crew stopped calling him a boy. His bold leadership and fearless fighting had made him a young man in their eyes. The pirates sailed away with abundant loot, spirits high after their triumph. That evening, the top fighters gathered in the captain's quarters to drink and play cards. The Young Man sat among them, heart light, watching the quartermaster deal with practiced ease. As the game wore on, the cabin door creaked open and the quartermaster's son peeked in, eyes wide. It was rare to have children aboard, but he was part of the crew, helping with chores when he could. The kid said nothing, just stared. The quartermaster caught his gaze, smiled, and beckoned him closer. The child scrambled onto his father's lap, barely able to contain his joy. He didn't know the rules, only that they were playing together. Every card became a shared triumph as his father whispered strategies, guiding their hands as one. The child beamed with pride, knowing he belonged.

On January 8, 2020, in West Palm Beach, I gave my life to God, confessing Jesus as Lord and believing in His resurrection. The Holy Spirit flooded my soul, and I cried for the first time in over a decade. God broke the chains that had bound me. Although I was filled with a mix of joy and fear. I didn't like calling Him *Father*. That word carried too much mistrust. I thought I had to surrender everything to Him at once, but that felt terrifying after so much broken trust with people. Then God gently whispered, *How about you just give Me one card? Watch Me play it and win. Then give Me another when you're ready.* So He built trust with me, card by card: relationships, career, finances. Slowly, I relaxed, watching Him orchestrate victories I never could have managed on my own. Over time, I realized He designed the game; of course, He knows how to win. And with every card I handed Him, I felt more joy and learned how to rest in His love.

Matthew 11:28-30

SCURVY

Pirates were skilled in many things, but cooking wasn't one. For nearly a year, the crew survived on nothing but potatoes; dry, flavorless, without butter or salt. At first, the Young Man gagged with every bite, but over time, he learned to stomach it. Still, he longed for more. A sprinkle of spice, a slice of bread, anything. But the crew spent their gold on repairs and port lizards, not food. Eventually, men fell ill: bleeding gums, weakness, fatigue. It was scurvy. The Young Man, recalling health lessons from his mother back on the farm, spoke up. Potatoes could sustain them for a while, he explained, but without fruit, like oranges, they would waste away. The captain listened, surprised by the Young Man's steady voice and knowledge. He ordered the ship back to Port Royal to restock. The crew cheered. But the Young Man's stomach twisted. Port Royal was the last place he wanted to go. What if the peg-legged man was still alive? What would he say? A wave of guilt hit. For the first time... he truly regretted his actions.

My whole life, I managed without God: filling my days with work, friends, and passions. But over time, it all began to feel bland, like eating plain baked potatoes just because everyone else was doing it. I didn't even realize how starved I was until I got sick with emptiness. Then I discovered God was the missing seasoning; the one who brings life flavor. With Him, the ordinary became extraordinary. Each moment felt rich and full, like tasting the meal I'd always longed for. When His Spirit filled my days, everything changed. Joy, meaning, and purpose overflowed in ways I'd never imagined. Before flying back to Michigan for my final semester of design school, the seven guys I'd lived with in Florida encouraged me to pray for godly friends. So I did. And to my amazement, God answered. Within a month, I had more solid friendships than ever before. That's when it hit me: I'm not powerless. I'm not alone. And everything doesn't depend on me after all.

John 10:10

RARE INVESTMENT

As they neared Port Royal, the quartermaster approached the Young Man at the helm and told him to follow. In the captain's quarters, he was stunned to find the captain pale and weak, barely clinging to life. The illness had taken its toll. In a raspy voice, the captain told him he was cherished by the crew, and that if he didn't survive the journey, he wanted the Young Man to become captain of the **Fearmonger.** *His jaw dropped. The quartermaster smiled, recognizing the rare honor being passed to one so young. But the Young Man's heart couldn't carry the weight of his lie. With trembling lips, he confessed how he had broken the peg-legged helmsman's leg to steal his place and lied about being his nephew. The quartermaster's smile vanished. He drew a pistol and pressed it to his head. Silence. The Young Man braced for death. Then the captain, after a long pause, spoke. He said he had invested too much in him to throw him away. That he had saved lives with his wisdom. Now, he must lead. The pistol lowered. The Young Man wept. The captain died as they entered port, and the Young Man became Captain.*

After all the people I'd hurt, the burdens I'd placed on others, and the harm I'd done to myself, God forgave a lost soul like me and chose to live in my heart. He let go of the ways I had wounded Him and stayed by my side. I'd spat in His face for years, yet He still wanted to be my friend. That wrecked me. I deserved rejection and death. But God looked at my mess and said, *I can work with this.* And that's what He began to do. Slowly, patiently, He started building something new from my shipwreck. I haven't had a serious injury or illness since meeting God, which amazes me because before that I had broken bones, undergone surgeries, needed stitches from a table saw accident, and battled chronic illnesses. His healing touch restored both my soul and my body.

Psalm 103:12

THE INVITATION

Word spread quickly about the young, new Captain as the ***Fearmonger*** *returned to Port Royal. Entering a tavern, the captain froze at the sight of a familiar figure: the peg-legged man in the corner. They locked eyes. Memories of their last hostile encounter flooded back, the moment they became sworn enemies. The Captain could hardly believe he was alive, and the tension was palpable. The old helmsman trembled, convinced the Captain would shoot him on the spot to end any threat of rivalry. The Captain walked toward him. The man raised his hands, pleading.* ***"Don't shoot."*** *The pub fell silent. All eyes watched as the Captain stopped in front of him. Instead of drawing a weapon, he extended his hand.* ***"I'm sorry,"*** *he said.* ***"Will you return to the Fearmonger as helmsman?"*** *The peg-legged man, stunned, began to weep with joy. No one expected mercy. After a pause, he clasped the offered hand. They embraced in the hushed stillness, both grateful for a second chance.*

Through childhood, being a Christian seemed to mean admiring God's beautiful ship from the docks, listening once a week to adventures it sailed 3,000 years ago. The gangplank connecting the dock to the ship represented scripture, yet instead of boarding, all I heard were endless arguments about its wood type, builder, and how it differed from every other gangplank. They argued head knowledge instead of crossing to sit with God in His captain's quarters and sail with Him. People felt too broken, undeserving, or afraid, like one-legged souls convinced He was too angry to welcome them. They treated the Bible like an idol, replacing relationship with information, doctrine, and debate because it was easier to study the gangplank than to actually board. But the gangplank isn't the destination; the Bible is an invitation. When I finally stepped aboard and sat with God, I began to truly know Him. His presence made me a better friend and a more forgiving soul in a way no amount of head knowledge could. What transformed me wasn't debate but the courage to cross and meet the One waiting inside.

2 Samuel 9:1-11

Cave Hospital

The Captain shared a meal with the peg-legged man, both eager to swap stories from the year apart. He laughed quietly when he saw the old sailor walking just fine. His shattered leg had fully healed. Grinning, the peg-legged man recounted that day on the hillside. He had lain for hours, certain he would die, until a passing priest found him and carried him to a cave. The priest tended him with quiet wisdom, setting the break, feeding him, and insisting he remain still for three months. Healing came slowly: leg in a splint, shaded from the sun, nourished daily, adjusted with care. The cave became a sanctuary. Recovery was just as vital as rescue. The captain listened in awe, struck by the miracle of it. In that moment, the two men bonded more deeply than ever. They had each been broken in different ways and returned not only alive, but better. From that meal forward, they pledged to remain comrades until death.

After spiritual heart surgery, I needed the same kind of recovery for my soul that a broken leg needs to heal. A powerful moment with God wasn't enough. I needed real recovery, or I'd be reinjured just as quickly as I was restored. A doctor once told me the number one cause of injuries in sports is lack of recovery. I realized the same is true for the soul. Just like muscles need time after workouts or injury, my spirit needed rest after a radical change. I needed the right environment: spiritual nutrition in gentle doses, godly friends, wise mentors, and long hours under the roofs of peace-filled homes. More than anything, I needed time to grow in the right direction. When people rushed in with too many corrections, it left me weary and confused. My heart was healing and couldn't bear pressure disguised as help. I'm grateful for those who trusted God to guide me, who knew when to speak and when to simply sit with me. The good news? Heaven's got the best hospitals. And I got the best care on Earth.

Psalm 147:3

FUEL

Once the sailors recovered from scurvy, the crew restocked the ship with a fully balanced supply of food. It had been maddening to cut the last voyage short just as the treasure hunt had reached its peak, and the death of the old captain had left the crew shaken. But the new Captain saw the lesson. A ship could have the finest sails, sharpest cannons, and strongest men, but without food, it was going nowhere. Food was the fuel. Without it, the men faded, and the ship became a drifting carcass of timber and iron. It amazed him how one small detail had nearly ended it all. Now, with barrels full and strength returning to every limb, the crew came alive again. Laughter echoed on the wind, and the spark of ambition reignited in their eyes. The ship groaned under full sail as if it, too, had awakened. With food in their bellies, gold in their eyes, and salt in their veins, the pirates were ready to rise again.

Now, imagine waking up in a world that shifts from black-and-white to vivid color. That's what life felt like after January 8, 2020. It wasn't just a date; it was the beginning of a new dimension of living. Each month afterward exploded with meaning. Ask me about any one of them, and I could tell story after story. Moments where God showed up in ways I never expected. Before that awakening, whole years passed without substance. I was like a ship adrift: polished, impressive even, but going nowhere because my crew had no food. That changed when the Holy Spirit became my daily nourishment. He fed every part of me, and suddenly I wasn't just afloat, I was moving with purpose. Life took on eternal weight. Instead of anxiety about the future, I leaned into it, ready to embrace every wave God would send. I wasn't just surviving. I was finally sailing. A pirate lives but once, yet if he lives bold and true, once is plenty.

John 6:35

DESERT BREEZE

The young Captain set out on his first mission, leading the ***Fearmonger*** *north to pillage untouched towns. After only hours of sailing, the wind vanished. The sea became a sheet of glass beneath the boiling Caribbean sun, and the ship halted. The crew grew restless, their excitement fading into complaining boredom. Sweat poured from their bodies, stinging their eyes. The Captain felt more lost than ever. All he had wanted was to impress them, to prove himself worthy of the title he had been given. Now, on his very first voyage, he had led them into stillness and heat, with no land in sight. He stood at the helm in silence, feeling the sun on his neck and the weight of every eye on board. A faint breeze would graze his cheek, stirring flickers of hope. But it never lasted. The sails hung limp, and the Captain stared at the horizon as the sun set, wondering if leadership was in him at all.*

Within the first few months of knowing God, two strangers prophesied over my life. I'd never met them, yet they spoke with startling accuracy about my private struggles and the future God had for me. It felt like they were reading my mail. And the things they said came to pass. I found myself wondering, *How can they hear God so clearly, and I cannot?* That question stirred a desperation in me to hear His voice. I began sacrificing space to listen. One wintry evening, overwhelmed by school and major family stress, I resisted turning to my usual crutches for relief, I drove to Lake Michigan during a blizzard. I walked the icy pier with ten-foot waves crashing around me and sat at the edge, telling God I wouldn't leave until He spoke. Within minutes, I heard Him. Clear, calming thoughts not my own, filled with peace and power. Tears filled my eyes as His voice felt like a breeze in the desert. From then on, the more space I made for Him, the more He spoke. He became my friend, and His words brought life.

Jeremiah 29:13

Sixth Sense

Seeing the Captain in quiet turmoil, the navigator stepped forward with a solution. He stood calm and confident while the captain wrestled with doubt. He advised angling the ship east and riding faint breezes for one mile, where a trade current would catch them and push the ship swiftly north. The Captain thought he was mad. Through his spyglass, the sea looked the same in every direction. But the navigator urged him to trust the advice, promising they'd escape the dead zone if they followed the plan. With no better idea, the Captain gave the order. Slowly, the ship crept eastward, nudged by the smallest breaths of wind. Until suddenly the hull lurched under a strong current. In an instant, they were moving north again. The crew erupted in cheers, but the Captain stood still, stunned. It felt like magic. The navigator explained that this part of the sea could stay windless for weeks, and without that current, they'd have been rowing endlessly. The young Captain realized every man on board had knowledge he lacked, and that true leadership meant learning to trust the wisdom around him.

Life with God sometimes feels like living in a mystery novel with a plot twist I never saw coming. Over time, I've realized that trusting Him is like developing a sixth sense, one that doesn't rely on what I can see, touch, or predict. Faith feels strange at first, because it often clashes with logic and the five senses I usually depend on. I can't smell provision on the horizon or see signs that a miracle is coming. Sometimes, I feel like I'm holding five loaves of bread and being asked to feed thousands. But I've learned to step forward anyway, even when nothing looks like progress. I've come to believe God is guiding me, even when He seems silent. His promises aren't void just because I can't see the fulfillment. His delay doesn't mean denial. His timing may be mysterious, but again and again, I've seen Him working behind the scenes, writing a story worth telling, far better than I ever imagined.

Isaiah 55:8-9

NATURE'S CHAINSAW

They found land in a place the navigator called Florida. After boating ashore on the eastern coast, the crew wandered through thick, marshy jungles of palm and mangrove. As they pushed through the foliage, they stumbled upon a beaver dam tucked beside a stream. The Captain had never heard of such a creature back in England, so they all paused to watch. The small animal moved with astonishing purpose, dragging branches larger than itself and placing them with precision. It seemed impossible that something so small could alter the course of a river, yet it did. The Captain observed that beavers were nature's quiet engineers, carrying out one of the most ambitious tasks in the wild. With sharp, tool-like teeth, they cut down trees, transforming the landscape with dams that fostered abundant new vegetation where other creatures could thrive. The Captain stood amazed. Something so tiny had managed to build, to bless, to change the world around it, one branch at a time.

Growing up, I saw my unique traits as obstacles. Dyslexia once made me feel isolated and convinced me I wasn't smart enough to chase big dreams. I quietly wrote off my childhood desire to become an inventor, believing people like me didn't do things like that. No one in my family had ever followed a path like Edison's, and I had no idea what it would take. I considered settling. But over time, I began to see that my struggles had shaped something rare in me: a different kind of mind, a superpower of relentless creativity, and the grit to solve problems others avoided. Like a beaver asking why it wasn't bigger for its job, I wondered why God had chosen me for such a challenging path. Yet I kept walking forward, and He met me at every step. I realized God's identity for me was to be an inventor who loves Jesus. Now, I find deep joy and purpose in using the gifts He gave me. God handed me a daunting mission, but with Him, the journey has become the most rewarding experience of my life.

Zechariah 4:10

PIRATE GOD

When the Captain first joined the crew, he was shocked. The pirates shouted over each other, bore scars like trophies, cracked crude jokes, and always seemed one wrong glance from betrayal. But over time, he began to see something more. These men were not just thieves; they were survivors. Many had lost everything, yet still rose to sing at sunrise. They laughed without holding back, forgave without pride, and worked like brothers when storms threatened to split the ship. They made no effort to hide their flaws, wearing them like salt-worn badges of grace. For all their noise and grit, they knew how to give. If you were hungry, they'd hand you the last scrap on their plate. They didn't wait to be perfect before they loved boldly. In their raw, untamed way, they lived with more honesty than most people he had ever known. They trusted, failed, tried again, and chased wonder without shame. Watching them, the Captain began to wonder if these messy, fearless men had discovered something the polished world had forgotten.

When I picture Jesus, I no longer see the pale, fragile figure from stained glass windows. I see a pirate captain, the good kind; bulging muscles and the type who steps aboard a broken vessel and loves them fiercely. He is rugged, with salt in his hair and kindness in his eyes. He laughs loudly, speaks plainly, and sails calmly through storms that terrify everyone else. Like the captain in the parable, Jesus saw something worth redeeming in the loud, messy crew of humanity. He wasn't afraid of their scars, shouting, or past. He came not to condemn the ship but to sail with it, teaching it how to love again. I used to think Jesus only liked the polished, the ones who never swore or doubted. But I've come to know Him as a captain who gives away His last meal, forgives quickly, sings with the broken, and eats with rogues. He is the fearless, generous, truth-speaking captain of this wild, sacred voyage. And following Him has been the greatest adventure of my life.

Luke 19:10

WAR STORIES

Peg Leg was a masterful storyteller. His tales from decades of sailing under the former captain pulled listeners in like a tide, placing them in the heart of each quest. The crew would gather around him, hanging on every word. Even the rowdiest pirates fell silent when he spoke. The new Captain often wondered at how these same men who trembled during real battles now laughed and cheered at stories of cannon fire and blood. Why did terror in the moment transform into joy in the retelling? He realized the answer lay in the outcome. The stories were thrilling because the audience knew they ended in triumph; the danger became entertainment only when seen from the safety of hindsight. But what if that same confidence could be felt amidst the fight itself, with the crew believing they would make it through? The captain wondered how life could be if they fought not with fear but with the certainty of victory already written.

When I first started inventing my music tool, an electronic pocket producer that helps artists quickly sketch their sound, everything felt wildly uncertain, like stepping into a high-stakes adventure where anything could go wrong. Fear creeps in when I forget that my own ending is good and that God already knows it. After university, I remember walking to the mailbox to send a $4,000 check to a law firm to file my first patent when I got a call from Marc, a guy I had met once in a cafe six months earlier. We had not spoken since. In a 60-second call, he said, *"God told me you're going through a risky exchange. He wants to protect you from a lawyer trying to scam you. A better door is coming."* Then he hung up. That same day, I got connected to a better lawyer and learned the first firm was a scam. Now, instead of fearing the fight, I hold metaphorical "faith watch parties" when impossible battles come my way, asking friends to join me in prayer as we watch God victoriously break down walls.

Romans 8:28

GIANTS AHEAD

After a long day exploring and marveling at the beaver, the crew gathered around the fire, and Peg Leg began to speak. But tonight, his story was different. He shared something he had heard from the priest who cared for him while he healed in the cave, a Bible story about David. David, Peg Leg said, was an outcast like them. He had been forgotten by his own father as a boy when a prophet came to anoint the next king. But God chose him anyway. At just fifteen, David was promised the crown, yet he wasn't given a throne, only a sling and a giant to kill. Then he spent the next fifteen years running for his life from King Saul. And yet he kept going, trusting God would come through. When David finally became king, he ruled with empathy and strength, having known what it felt like to suffer. Peg Leg looked around the fire and told the crew they were not so different. They had also been broken, overlooked, and chased, but their reward would come if they stayed strong. The men roared, ready to find more treasure.

God called me to be an inventor. But instead of a throne of award-winning ideas off the bat, I was handed hard situations that forced me to build trust first. After graduating top of my class in industrial design, I expected to launch my dream design career in Grand Rapids. But while listening for God's voice, He told me to move to West Palm Beach, Florida, a place with no design jobs. It made no sense. My parents had helped with tuition. My professors believed in me. I was leaving behind the best friends I'd ever made. Loneliness was my biggest fear, but God whispered, *"I gave you friends in Michigan. I'll provide again. Trust the story I'm writing."* Like David facing a giant with only a sling and a promise, I sold my car, moved with no job, and bet everything on God's voice. It felt risky. But it became the best decision of my life.

1 Samuel 17:45

Bōld Bees

During their weeks exploring Florida, the Captain found his mind drifting back to childhood on the farm, where he watched honeybees buzzing around their hives. He remembered one behavior in particular: the waggle dance. When a bee discovered a patch of nectar, it would return and perform a precise dance to show the others where to go. Most of the colony would follow. But a few ignored the dance and ventured off on their own. It was those curious few who sometimes found even better nectar and helped the entire hive thrive. The Captain saw his crew in those bees. While most pirates followed the same tired trade routes south or west, they had sailed north into the unknown. For weeks, they'd found little. Some men grew restless. But the Captain held on to hope. Maybe they weren't lost. Maybe they were explorers, bold enough to go where others had not. And just maybe, like those bees, they were about to stumble onto something no one else had found.

When I moved to Florida, I felt like a honeybee venturing into wildflowers, leaving the beaten path, even the one most Christians stick to. I had no job, no plan, and no nearby friends. I cried out to God in the loneliness, and He asked me a question: *If I provide the people, will you gather them?* I said *yes*. The next day, God flooded my life with connection; five to ten new faces each day. Within months, I knew hundreds. Somehow, I had a presence in nearly every circle, which was wild considering I usually prefer solitude. Then He nudged me to host a worship night. I didn't play guitar, and I'd never sung publicly. I said yes again; 45 people came, and His Spirit moved. From there: beach frisbee tournaments with a hundred people, worship bonfires, fire-spinning lessons, dinners in my apartment, even baptizing friends in the ocean. God had asked me to trust Him in the unknown. I did. And like a bold bee straying from the dance, I found nectar where no one else thought to look.

Hebrews 11:8

HOLD TIGHT

As they hacked through Floridian jungles, Peg Leg shared another story he'd heard from the priest. It was about a man named Moses, tasked with something as impossible as a beaver stopping a river. God told him to lead two million people out of slavery in Egypt. Against all odds, they escaped. But the Egyptian army came charging after them, full of fury. With nowhere to turn, Moses reached the sea. Water stretched endlessly before them. Death followed behind. What must he have thought, with people screaming at his back, no way forward in sight? But Moses had one thing left: God's promise. Not a map or step-by-step plan. Just a word to keep moving forward. So he did. And only when they reached the sea's edge did it split, not before. Peg Leg paused and looked at the men. ***"We're like Moses,"*** *he said,* ***"Walking through an unknown land with no clear answers. But if we trust the dream and keep walking, the path will appear."*** *The crew nodded, spirits lifted, and kept moving forward.*

God led me into freelance videography in Florida, a field for which I had no passion. Though I was trained in product design and felt this work wasted my gift, He didn't give me my dream job but instead placed me in something I dreaded, teaching me to do it with peace and joy as an offering. I learned to fail forward and eventually found myself loving it, overflowing with joy in work I wasn't even gifted at. In time, I led a film team for a major AI summit in Miami, but after submitting my invoice, the company declared bankruptcy, leaving me unpaid. Barely scraping by, I then felt God call me to join a two-week mission in Poland to help launch JH Outback University retreats, so I bought the ticket on credit. Within days, donations poured in, more than double what I needed. Like Moses walking into the sea with only a promise, I learned that obedience may not make sense at first, but the path always opens when God says move.

Psalm 23:5

HONEYMOON

Peg Leg continued the story, explaining how, after Moses led his people out of Egypt, magically parting the Red Sea, God guided them through the wilderness for 40 years, providing bread from the sky and water from unexpected places. It wasn't just survival; it was learning to trust God and each other, even in a barren land. Similarly, this crew now wandered through the swamp, learning dependence amid uncertainty. To an outsider stumbling upon them, deep in uncharted jungles, it might look foolish. They might be called lost pirates, surviving on bugs and grit. The effort could appear absurd: an aimless band of misfits. But what lies just beyond sight might change everything. More was being built than what the eye can see: trust, brotherhood, and the kind of strength only hardship can forge. Like the people of Moses, these sailors were not lost. They were being shaped. And when the moment was right, the reward would come. Until then, they moved forward through the unknown, one determined step at a time.

When I first encountered God, my life changed drastically. He stripped away my job and financial security, not to punish me, but to build my trust. For years, He led me from Michigan to Florida, then to work at JH Ranch in California, then to Poland, launching retreats and beyond. I had no roadmap, just His voice guiding me one step at a time. Many churchgoers questioned my choices, assuming I was lost or misled. But I knew I was learning to follow divine wisdom, not human logic. It often felt like wandering through a desert, yet just as God provided bread from heaven and water from rocks, He met my needs in the most surprising ways. That season became a hidden treasure, a honeymoon with God where trust was my daily bread. I learned to walk with joy, shielded from discouragement, knowing I was a son of the King. What looked foolish to others was sacred ground to me. I was not lost. I was being shaped. And God always showed up, proving I was never alone.

Deuteronomy 8:2

ANCHORLESS

Hearing the stories of Moses reminded the Captain of a time he had served as helmsman under the previous captain during a hurricane. The storm was fierce; waves towered 20 feet high, rigging broke, and panic swept the deck. Without asking, the Boy threw the anchor overboard, thinking it was their only hope of avoiding being blown miles off course or dashed against island rocks. But the anchor rope snapped, and he quickly learned it was a costly mistake. Anchoring in a storm, the old captain later taught, is often the worst choice. Better to roll with the waves than lose what matters most. The Boy had once believed survival meant control, coming up with ten possible solutions in a crisis. But time and again, the old captain offered an eleventh, an option that seemed painful or reckless but proved the only true path to safety. It taught the boy that survival isn't always common sense. Sometimes, what feels like chaos is the very force that moves a ship exactly where it needs to go.

During my season of learning trust, God asked me to temporarily surrender something I never expected: romantic relationships. Giving up money and career dreams was hard, but the idea of long-term singleness felt unbearable. I'd believed real manhood meant success, income, and having a beautiful woman by your side. But God began to show me I could be strong without any of those things. I gave Him five years of singleness, and during that time, He became my closest companion. He also healed a long-standing pornography addiction through a nine-month accountability program called Freedom Fight. It was brutal, filled with discomfort and sacrifice. But I found freedom, brotherhood, and peace. Eventually, I even mourned the day I'd meet my wife, knowing it would shift the sweet intimacy I had with God. But I heard God promising a partner far beyond anything I could have imagined; a woman whose deep love for Him would only draw me closer to the heart of the One I love most.

Hebrews 6:19

PRO WRESTLER

While exploring the Florida coast beaches, the crew often spent their free time wrestling in the sand. It started as a way to grow stronger and stay sharp for future raids, but it quickly became something more. Each match built strength, coordination, and trust. Wins were thrilling, and losses stung, but both shaped the fighters into more skillful men. Every grapple taught a lesson, every fall a moment to rise again. Over time, the crew grew closer, laughing, bleeding, and learning together. Whether standing tall in victory or brushing off defeat, each man became sharper because of the other. And when the matches ended, the whole crew cheered, not just for the winner, but for the bond being built between them.

After returning from Poland, God called me to move to Nashville to help revive the city. It felt impossible. I knew almost no one there, had no job lined up, and no car to make the journey. I didn't want to leave Florida, but I wrestled with God in tears, saying, *"If You want me in Nashville, You will need to provide a vehicle. P.S. I've always wanted an old Toyota truck."* The next morning, I met a man at a 6:30 a.m. men's group selling a 2003 Tundra with 57,000 miles for $10,000. I had no money, but I kept praying, wrestling with God through more tears. People mocked me for not just buying a flight, but I was willing to look foolish if God did not come through. Days later, I received a call from someone out of state who said God told them to give me $10,000 anonymously. I bought the truck and drove to Nashville in a hurricane. That miracle taught me that wrestling with God is not weakness; it's relationship. Just like wrestling sharpens fighters, so too do I grow through wrestling with my Maker, growing closer in struggle instead of trying harder. I'm not anyone special to receive this much favor from God. I simply obey and trust that He will provide for all my needs.

Genesis 35:10

Prince of Happiness

Some of the crew grew restless without recent loot, but the Captain noticed something interesting: the worst arguments often came when bellies were full and rum was flowing. Yet in leaner times, when supplies and hopes ran low, they were kinder, more united. There was something sacred about unsatisfied sailors leaning on each other. Still, the Captain watched their provisions shrink and felt the pressure. Was he just a lost captain, drifting without purpose? He longed for a clear direction, a next conquest, but something in him hesitated. He was tired of seeing fear in the eyes of those they robbed. Tired of pretending stolen gold filled the ache inside. It never lasted. The sea was wide, but his vision for the future had never felt smaller. Was the dream of momentary happiness from scattered loot enough to sustain him?

A verse from Ecclesiastes always puzzled me. *"It is better to go to a house of mourning than to go to a house of feasting."* I used to chase the Western dream: get the job, find the girl, live happily ever after. But the more I studied Scripture, the more I saw it warned against comfort. Most sin crept in when things were easy, like drifting into a riptide without noticing. Solomon fell at the height of his kingdom. David's worst failure happened while resting in his palace. I started to see the same pattern in me. The stories that shaped history weren't written on mountaintops, but in valleys. Paul found peace in prison. David penned psalms while running for his life. And me? I found the deepest joy and clearest vision when I had no money, power, or plan; only desperate dependence on God. I had no consistent income and averaged a three-digit net worth for the first five years of knowing God, which taught me to stop striving and trust Him daily. Even in seasons of lack, I overflowed with peace that made no sense. Jesus isn't the prince of happiness; He's the Prince of Peace. This peace flows into my valleys like living water, restoring my soul.

Ecclesiastes 7:2

FŌRAGER

One day, deep in the inland swamps, a lone visitor surprised the crew. An indigenous man appeared, walking calmly without any supplies. He was friendly and spoke only a few words of English, which made the encounter peaceful, as there was nothing to steal and no threat to fear. Miles from any settlement, this man seemed completely at home. He carried no rations, tools, or weapons, yet moved with confidence. Through gestures and signs, the crew learned he didn't need gear because he had learned to live off the land. His ease in the wild puzzled the pirates, who were used to heavy packs, strict plans, and slow progress. They carried everything they might need, while this man carried only knowledge and trust. He foraged as he went, dancing through the woods, meeting hunger with his instincts. Everything he needed was already around him. With a smile, he motioned for them to follow him to his village. Curious, the crew agreed, stepping into the unknown.

For several months, I had immersed myself in the BEMA Discipleship podcast by Marty Solomon, exploring the Bible through an Eastern Rabbinic lens. The stories came alive in a way I had never experienced, and I found myself falling in love with Scripture. But the deeper I went, the more I realized I was missing a necessity: a community to discuss and explore the Bible with. I asked God to provide companions, and just days later, I stumbled upon a weekly BEMA group in Nashville. To my amazement, their upcoming meeting was on the exact episode I had just finished that day. After months of walking this journey alone, God connected me with others at the perfect moment. It reminded me of the forager, who carried no supplies yet walked with peace, collecting food along the way. That is how I began to see my own spiritual path. Legalism had felt like a heavy backpack, but this new way was different. I learned to move freely, trusting that when I needed spiritual food, God would provide it right around the corner.

Philippians 4:19

NEWBŌRN

The real reason the Captain agreed to visit the tribe was desperation. He hoped to gather intel on nearby settlements to raid or plunder. But the natives, though kind, had no riches, and the language barrier made questions useless. Still, something unexpected happened. For the first time in years, the pirates saw a newborn baby in the village. The crew fell silent, drawn to the tiny child, soft cheeks and wide eyes glowing with innocence. Hardened men cracked smiles, momentarily undone by the quiet beauty of new life. The baby's coos stirred something deeper than treasure. No one thought of the baby's future hardships, only the wonder of what he might become. But the Captain stayed quiet. He realized he saw his own life through a lens of failure and fear. But what if he viewed himself the way he looked at that baby, with wonder? With the hope that something beautiful might still grow from where he stood? They returned to the ship as the stars began to rise.

When I first moved to Nashville, I quickly slipped into fear and doubt. Why am I here? How could this turn into anything good? My life felt far from what I'd imagined as a kid. Instead of believing in miraculous success, I focused on my flaws and failures. I felt behind, like maybe I was just a mess-up, and my life might end like a dystopian film. That fear, that hopeless narrative, was exactly what the enemy wanted me to believe. But in those low moments, I began asking God how He sees me. His answer was always steady and kind. He reminded me that He's proud of me, that I'm worth spending time with, that I'm wonderfully made, and He wouldn't change a thing. My future, in His eyes, is still bright. I'm not late. I'm right on time. To this day, I ask Him if He's proud of me. And He always says yes. Seeing babies reminds me how to live with wonder towards my own life, and see myself with the same hope God has for me.

Matthew 18:3

Big Sound Little Bird

The Captain slept like a rock that night after days of swamp bushwhacking. But at dawn, he jolted awake to a blaring sound echoing through his quarters. Heart pounding, he nearly shrieked, sure the natives had returned with a war cry to attack. Rushing to the window, he found the shoreline calm and quiet. The sound came again, piercing the morning stillness as the sun rose over the sea. It echoed like a massive bird call, strange and unfamiliar. Startled, the captain burst onto the deck, scanning the rigging for nearly a minute for what he assumed must be some great sea bird. Then a third cry rang out, and he finally located the source. Perched on the ropes was a tiny bird, no larger than a cricket ball. He stared, stunned, as it chirped once more; clear, sharp, and impossibly loud, before fluttering off. The Captain stood frozen, wondering how something so small could carry such a mighty voice across the sea.

Looking back on my time in Florida, some of the things God led me to do felt like failures. I rented out a coworking venue to host a premiere night for the first song I wrote, called *Embrace*. It was going perfectly… until the smoke machines triggered the fire alarms. The fire department showed up, and I was kicked out. Later, I planned a larger event called *Creative Courtyard*, a local music festival where I was set to headline with a custom techno set. Months of prep, big dreams, expecting hundreds of guests. And only 60 people came due to a basic ticketing mistake. I lost money and felt like I'd failed again. But God used it all. Each setback taught me something I needed for the next chapter in Nashville. God was teaching me to smile through the valleys like lifting weights, building strength. Now, like that tiny bird facing the unknown, I sing a beautiful song boldly, not because I'm strong, but because I trust the One who is. Each trial becomes a dawn chorus of praise, declaring God's goodness even when I feel small.

Matthew 6:25-34

DOWN FEATHER

After the startling bird encounter, the Captain began dressing as the sun rose. His bed was topped with the comfort of a soft down pillow they had claimed in a past raid. While fastening his belt, he noticed a tiny feather on the floor, which had escaped from the pillow. The room was silent and still, yet the feather began to stir. It lifted and spun slowly in place, caught in an unseen current, as if moved by something more than air. The Captain stared, entranced, as it danced across the wooden floor with quiet purpose in an invisible tornado. It moved like it knew something none of the other furniture did.

In Michigan and Florida, I had spent years diligently developing my patent-pending music invention, which had won multiple state-wide pitch competitions, all while believing Nashville was the perfect launchpad. But just days after arriving, God gave me a random blueprint for a music documentary pilot: create a hit song in 30 days by collaborating with a global audience through polls and soundbites. That same day, a family offered me their home for three months, exactly the time I'd committed to the project. Even more miraculously, a couple already renting there was also working on a documentary. I prayed for a music producer, and God provided my friend Dan, who moved to Nashville to collaborate. With almost no network, over 600 people joined our newsletter. God provided exactly 20 musicians. Five singers, five producers, five songwriters, and five instrumentalists; all gifted and God-fearing. When we needed high-end cameras, someone offered their $10,000 camera setup. I had promised God I would share His miracles if He gave us a stage. In faith, we booked the 300-seat Franklin Theatre without funds. Two days before payment was due, someone anonymously paid the $4,000. We nearly sold out. That night, we shared every testimony, bringing tears and conversations that glorified God. Now streaming as 'We the Music Documentary,' it reminds me that nothing is wasted when I follow God's voice as sensitive as a feather at the slightest hint of wind.

John 3:8

...FINDS GREAT TREASURE...

What now?

Matthew 13:44

The Captain had no idea what surprise awaited him that day. Without a clear direction for the crew, he wandered to the shore and began wrestling matches with his men to pass the time. Mid-grapple, his heel struck something solid in the sand. Brushing it away revealed a large, weathered chest with a key already in the lock. Heart racing, he opened it to find the largest pile of gold coins he had ever seen. No name, no trap, no blood to be spilled... just forgotten treasure. He laughed and cried at the same time, overwhelmed by the absurd kindness of it all. It had to be the treasure from the old childhood legends, the one everyone thought was hidden atop a distant mountain. But the clues had been misunderstood. It was here, ***where the sky unfolds above a quiet beach, under the sun, and footprints vanish in the sand.*** *For the first time, he saw abundance that didn't require force. Maybe this was his true rite of passage. He no longer needed to take; he had freely received.*

I had been giving God pieces of my life cautiously, like rationing trust. But what if I leaned my full weight into Him? I had seen Him provide friends in a city where I feared I would be lonely, a truck when I needed one, and a documentary team that sold out a theater. Still, I'd never seen someone go all-in. So I asked Him, *"How far can this go?"* and heard Him whisper, *"As deep as you want. Just try Me and see how good I am."* So I dove. And I found treasure. I stopped hustling, treading water, grabbing at passing blessings. Instead, I sat beside Him on the riverbank, letting Him show me where provision gathers, ready to wade in at the right time. I was still a spiritual pirate with needs, but instead of stealing from others, I let God fill me until I overflowed. And once I saw who He truly was willing to be for me, I never wanted to go anywhere without Him again.

John 17:3

BEACH TREASURE

The Captain, rich beyond belief, had nothing left to prove. He turned his ship south toward a distant island with towering cliffs, hoping for a better vantage point for the journeys ahead. Excitement pulsed through the crew as they docked longboats to begin the brutal climb. The mountain twisted upward, legs burned, water ran low, and some questioned if the view was worth it. But at the peak, all doubt vanished. A breathtaking cliff stretched out before them, overlooking the endless ocean. The wind cooled their sweat-soaked skin and silenced their chatter. They stood at the edge, stunned and speechless. The view was staggering, but so was the drop. Each man felt the tremble of fear just beneath the wonder. They understood how thin the line was between beauty and danger. But it was worth it. Together, they scanned the horizon to see where their next great journey might begin.

I used to think prayer was mostly asking God for favors and reading Scripture. But I've come to see it as an ongoing, two-way conversation. God isn't withholding. If I'm not hearing Him, something is blocking me from listening. He's a good Father who longs to speak to His kids. I started noticing that people who truly walk with God (prophetic, unpredictable types whose wild-card hearts once made me uncomfortable because I couldn't fit them into a box) were often the ones who loved the best and bore the most fruit. They stirred in me a hunger to hear God in every moment. Jamie Winship teaches to start with truth-telling: bring God my fears, doubts, even my anger. He can handle it. Then ask two questions: *"God, what do You want me to know?"* and *"What do You want me to do?"* That posture moves me from complaint to communication. Pursuing intimacy with God feels like climbing a cliff. It's focused. Humbling. But the view is worth it. At the top, I glimpse His beauty, power, and kindness. And in that place, I hear His voice. I believe every human being can hear God speak. It just takes the climb.

Psalm 42:1

COASTAL CLIFFS

From the cliff, the Captain gazed across the horizon. His thoughts drifted to his family he left behind; still tilling the same soil and clinging to the comfort of routine, never tasting adventure. He wondered if they were truly content or if some part of them longed for more. A soft ache stirred in his chest, not regret for leaving, but sorrow that they had never dared to step beyond the edge of their known world. Fear had kept them anchored to the land while he had found something they never would: the wild joy of braving the waves, of stumbling upon treasure beyond belief, of walking through danger with the greatest band of brothers he could have imagined. These moments, the laughter, risk, and freedom, were worth every storm and sleepless night. As the sea stretched endlessly before him, he knew he had chosen right.

After I found the Treasure and gave up everything to walk closely with God, a strange sorrow settled in. It wasn't grief for what I had lost, but for those around me who claimed to know Him yet lived anchored to routines, clinging to safety, their eyes dimmed by a weight they could not name. Their true potential was held back by the walls around their comfort zone. They spoke of faith, but their hearts had never sailed beyond the shore. Some tried to calm my passion, calling it a phase or a passing high, but their voices trembled with something deeper, fear, envy, maybe even regret. I had stepped into the life they always talked about but never dared to live, and I could feel how uncomfortable that made them. Not because I judged them, but because my fire reminded them of a fire they still longed for. I had lived in both worlds. I knew what waited beyond the edge. Freedom. Joy. Peace that made every storm worthwhile. And now, I want nothing more than for them to taste it too. But to taste it, they would have to leave the shore.

Matthew 16:25

LANDLŌCKED

Despite his family's lack of desire for adventure, there was still much he'd learned from them. What he cherished most was their love for each other. No matter how tired the day left them, they always made time for a dinner date. He remembered his father straightening his collar and his mother smiling in a fresh dress, both eager just to be together. They never let routine dull their affection. His father always found the words to tell her how beautiful she looked, and her laughter soon filled the room. Even when tension lingered from the day, they'd gently talk it through so nothing spoiled the warmth of their night. They held hands, shared stories, and protected their joy. That kind of love was rare, love that chose presence over performance.

I began to treasure intimacy with God more than just signs and wonders or the spiritual *"hookup culture."* It wasn't about chasing spiritual thrills or having transactional encounters, but simply being with Him like true friends do. I discovered how to meet with God each day in a way that opened a miraculous space of connection, so rich I couldn't help but linger in it. I start by entering His presence with praise and gratitude, then invite the Holy Spirit to reveal anything standing in the way of our closeness: unforgiveness, pride that fed fear, the lust of the flesh that searched for peace in lesser things, or the lust of the eyes that stirred jealousy and discontentment. As I lay those down and plead the blood of Jesus to silence every accusation from the enemy, I am free to speak with the Father without shame. True repentance simply means turning away from sin and returning to a close, intimate relationship with Him. I am not begging for blessings or stuck in the past. I am listening and talking with Him. I ask what is written in my book of life for the day, and He shows me. I write it down, follow His lead, and watch miracles unfold. Simple. Beautiful. Not a performance. Not a transaction. A relationship.

Psalm 139:16

DATE

After vowing to share the treasure freely, the Captain noticed a remarkable shift in his crew. He had promised to pay them handsomely, and something changed in their eyes. The grumbling and hesitation that sometimes slowed their work vanished. Every command he gave was met with immediate action. No dragging feet. The men moved like a single, well-trained unit, bound not just by duty but by a shared trust. The Captain no longer needed to raise his voice; he simply spoke, and they listened. Even when a command seemed strange or unclear, they followed without hesitation, believing fully that their leader had their best interests in mind. They were no longer a crew chasing riches. They were a brotherhood, united by a generous captain who had chosen to lift them with his fortune rather than hoard it. The treasure was changing their hearts.

Hearing God's voice prompting me to do small, seemingly random things was strange early on. *Hug that person. Give that gift. Say this one sentence to a friend today.* Sometimes I obeyed, and beautiful things happened. But a few times, I chose not to obey, brushing it off as too small or inconvenient. Moments later, I would watch someone nearby do the very thing God had asked of me. It was humbling. God spoke, *"Parker, I don't need you, but I want to use you. If you won't obey, I will send someone else."* That moment changed everything. I realized He was building trust in the small things to entrust me with more. From then on, I committed to radical obedience, even when it made me look foolish. And there was a cost. I lost what looked like dream jobs and dream relationships. But over time, God began to restore what I had lost and blessed me in ways I never imagined. I had joined the ranks of those who obey not just out of duty, but because they trust their Captain. Now, I honor his voice, and even when nothing visible changes, I have peace knowing that I've followed orders to the best of my ability.

Luke 16:10

Quick Ears

One morning while sailing through uncharted islands, the Captain woke early and made his way to the quarterdeck to take in the surrounding beauty. As he stood in the quiet of dawn, his eyes caught something unusual near the center of the ship. There, sprouting through the cracks in the worn floorboards, was a single upright red rose. He squinted, certain it had not been there the day before. The deck was swabbed daily, trampled by boots, and scorched by relentless sun, yet somehow this delicate flower had taken root and bloomed. He stepped closer, marveling at how something so fragile had survived in such a harsh and unlikely place. With no soil, no shade, and no care, it had pressed through the wood and reached for the sky. Beauty broke through where it should not have existed.

God led me through valley after valley, into seasons so dark and painful they should have crushed me. Each month brought new trials, more pressure, and harder tests, yet something unexplainable was growing inside me. More joy. More peace. More strength. Not the kind the world gives, but something deeper, something anchored. As I continued to radically obey God, people around me, both in the world and the church, began to take notice. They could not understand how I was still standing, let alone thriving, like a delicate rose springing from the deck of a ship where boots trample daily and the sun burns without mercy. I had no natural reason to flourish, but I did. Because in the heart of every battle, God prepared a table for me to sit and feast with Him in the presence of my enemies. And the more I dined with Him, the more others grew curious and wanted in. When I got wounded in the spiritual fight, I would return to Him, and He would restore my soul. Heaven truly does have the best hospitals.

Philippians 4:12

SHIP FLOWER

After a few days of exploring nearby islands, the crew docked in Tortuga to resupply and scrape the barnacles from the hull. Spirits were high as they landed, eager for fresh goods, hot meals, and a break from the sea. The Captain strolled through the bustling streets with his mates, breathing in the scent of salt and spice. He instinctively reached into his pocket to check for the treasure chest key. His fingers met nothing. His heart jumped. He patted his belt, checked his coat, then every fold of fabric again. Still nothing. A wave of panic surged through him as fear gripped his chest. ***Had someone stolen it? Was their fortune gone?*** *Without saying a word, he turned and sprinted back toward the docks, weaving through crowds, lungs burning, and mind spinning. He burst aboard the ship, scrambled into the hold, and there it was, the key, sitting casually atop the chest, right where he had left it. Forgotten, untouched, and miraculously still there. Relief washed over him as he sank down, breath ragged, heart pounding. The treasure was safe, but he would never forget his key again.*

Once I came to know God deeply, I learned the hard way what happened when I tried to go without Him. On the days I rushed into work or busyness without first connecting with Him, everything unraveled. I felt anxious, off-balance, and disoriented, like going through withdrawals after God had become my lifeline, my compass, my peace, and I had nothing else to lean on. Starting days without my treasure chest key, I would scramble through the chaos of my day, only to realize what I had forgotten. And when I finally paused and returned to that quiet place of communion, I found Him still there, waiting. Untouched. Patient. Ready to guide and restore. He truly is the key, the one that unlocks peace in confusion, strength in weakness, and companionship in every storm. I cannot afford to forget Him. In a world of endless distraction, He is not just important. He is essential.

Luke 15:8–10

LOST KEY

That evening, with a belly full and the sound of crew shanties echoing softly from the deck, the Captain settled into his chair and gazed at the gentle glow of the lamp in his quarters. Something about it held him still. Lamps, he thought, were quiet companions, never demanding attention, just offering their warmth in silence. They rested humbly on tables in soft, neutral tones, content simply to exist. There was no rush in their presence, no urgency, only an invitation to slow down, to breathe, to pick up a pencil and sketch something for the joy of it. In a world full of noise and motion, this little lamp lived differently. It reminded him that peace could still be found in small, steady things.

Before I knew God, I used to be a slave to my work, hustling seven days a week without a break. I'm a hard worker, and that got me far in life, at a high cost of severe burnout. But when I became a son of the King, God told me I was no longer a slave. His report says I deserve a Sabbath day that He will bless. A day where I stop working, stop worrying, and simply rest. I can enjoy the things I love: good food with friends, video games, music, and most importantly, Him. I now take Sabbath from Friday sundown to Saturday sundown, and it's my favorite day of the week. I work hard six days, then I cannonball into the soothing hot tub of Sabbath rest. An opportunity to step back and take it all in. It's not always easy to break the momentum of a busy week and trust that God will provide, but He's never failed me. Sabbath reminds me of the posture of a lamp, content, peaceful, and intimate with God. I like to call it *"aggressive lamping,"* the intentional practice of resting fully in God's presence. When I was not aggressively lamping, I was missing out. It's a beautiful rhythm of life, a reminder that I'm not a slave to work but a child of God, invited to rest in His provision every day.

Galatians 4:7

AGGRESSIVE LAMPING

While resupplying in the bustling market of Tortuga, the crew wandered among stalls filled with spices, fruits, and fresh catches from the sea. At one stall, local fishermen stood proudly over their display, chatting about the morning's haul. Among the catch was a large tuna. The fishermen explained how it lived in the deep and never stopped moving, needing to swim constantly to breathe. Over a meal of fresh raw tuna, the crew pondered the curious ways of this relentless creature of the deep.

When I moved to Nashville, I felt the weight of uncertainty pressing on me. How would I afford housing in a city where rent climbs higher every year? I had no money and no plan. It would have been easy to slip into endless hustle, chasing solutions like a tuna that must swim without stopping, just to breathe. But instead of racing, I chose to trust God fully, letting Him guide me to green pastures and quiet waters that restore my soul. I stopped striving and started obeying, and God began to provide in ways that could only be called miraculous. Every few months, someone would approach me and say God had told them to offer me their home while they traveled. This happened again and again, until I realized I had been given free housing for three years in this expensive city without ever asking. Even services and products would come my way like gifts, freely offered without request. Free printing at Staples, complimentary meals at restaurants, unexpected gifts from the Apple Store, sunglasses handed to me, gas pumps already paid for, free chiropractic care, even random checks in the mail. And these weren't from wealthy donors. They came from average, middle-class people, the kind who simply listened to God's prompting and gave generously. Generosity followed me wherever I went. God made a way where there was no way. I didn't have to earn it. I simply had to lean into my worth as His beloved child and trust Him to provide.

Psalm 127:1

TUNA

One quiet afternoon, the Captain set out to stretch his legs with his new companion, a Portuguese Water Dog that had once belonged to the old captain before being passed down after his death. The dog had a loyal heart and a spark in his eyes, and in no time, the two had formed a bond stronger than the strongest rope on the ship. While ashore, they would walk the hills surrounding Tortuga together, side by side. The Captain often marveled at how the dog never questioned the path ahead. With no concern for destination or danger, the dog bounded forward with joy, thrilled to simply follow. He had no map, no plan, yet trusted fully that wherever the captain led, it would be good, because they would face it together. It struck the Captain deeply. The dog was not chasing scenery or treasure. He was content just to journey with his master.

I used to crave detailed blueprints for my future, convinced everything would collapse without a clear plan. I wanted certainty to avoid daily dependence and seasons of confusion, but now I've found peace not in knowing every step, but in trusting God the way a joyful dog trusts its master. God may not reveal the full plan, but He walks with me and will never leave. I realized that if man does not live on bread alone but on every word from God, I should spend more time feeding my spirit than my body. So I set out to walk and talk with God for roughly three hours daily and have done that ever since, replacing my usual devotions with long conversations in nature, three walks a day, an hour each, without my Bible, simply journaling what He spoke to me: the first at 5 a.m., the second after lunch, and the third before bedtime. Everything began to shift. My work bore more fruit with less effort, and after a lifetime of restless nights, I finally slept in perfect peace. God gave rest to His beloved, just as He promised.

Psalm 127:2

A Dog's Heart

While exploring the jungles near Tortuga, the Captain and his dog came upon a quiet river and sat down on the bank. As the sun broke through the clouds, a group of turtles emerged from the water and climbed onto nearby logs to bask in the light. The Captain watched, captivated by their stillness. They, too, did not fret about potential storms, falling trees, or predators. They simply existed, calm and unbothered, soaking in the sun. There was no urgency in their movements, no anxiety in their eyes, only a quiet trust in the world around them. The Captain realized they were not foolish for their peace. They trusted their shells to protect them and believed that even if the river carried them far from home, they would find a new place to belong. Their presence spoke of a wisdom that needed no words. In their stillness, they reminded him to slow down, breathe, and welcome the moment instead of fearing what might come.

For most of my life, I thought a prince's royalty came from his palace, riches, and guards, that his power depended on what surrounded him. But then I wondered, if that prince were taken captive in a foreign land, stripped of his wealth and robes, would he still be royal? The answer is *yes*. His identity comes not from what he has, but from whose he is. Even without outward signs, his captors would know he belongs to a greater kingdom. I realized the same is true for me. My royalty as a son of the King of the universe does not depend on my bank account, clothes, or circumstances. Like the turtles basking calmly on a riverbank, I can rest in peace, knowing I am protected and provided for no matter where life carries me. They did not worry about storms or dangers. They trusted their shells, just as I now trust God. When I stop striving and simply rest in His care, I find a peace that not only strengthens me but spills over to others, spreading light and life wherever I go.

John 14:27

TURTLES

Recalling Peg Leg's story of David slaying the giant with a single stone, the Captain felt a spark of inspiration to learn the ancient skill of slinging. Wading into the river, he began searching for smooth stones. As he picked up a few in his hand, he was struck by their spherical polish, their quiet perfection. These stones had once been jagged, raw, and sharp, but the river had shaped them over time without force or struggle. A craftsman might spend weeks chiseling away at a rock, each strike leaving new edges and deeper wear on the hands. Even with sandpaper and precision, the result often fell short. Yet here, the water had done in time what no tool could. It had smoothed them gently, effortlessly, through constant flow and quiet persistence. The Captain stared at the stones and understood. Some things are not shaped by willpower or force. Some are shaped by surrender, by time, and by letting go.

For a long time, I felt frustrated watching my Floridian friend Daniel being discipled by an older man named Randy. While I was hustling to read book after book, filling journals, and pushing myself to grow spiritually, Daniel and Randy simply spent time together. They talked, laughed, and rested in life. Randy was teaching Daniel how to be held in God's embrace, how to be fathered by the King, while I was scraping and bruising myself through endless spiritual effort, trying to earn what they freely received. I thought I would win the race by working harder, but over time, I saw the opposite. Daniel and Randy bore fruit without trying, blessing everyone they met. Their lives left a gentle wake of peace that I could not manufacture. Just like jagged rocks that become smooth not by force, but by resting in the flow of a river. The sharp edges of my life began to wear away, too, not through striving, but through resting in Father's embrace. When I stopped fighting and let God's love shape me, peace and fruit came naturally, without effort or strain.

Psalm 46:4

RIVER STŌNES

The Captain commanded the crew to leave Tortuga and sail south to explore the Southern Spanish Main. By now, he had spent so much time with them that they could recognize his voice in any setting. Even in the loudest pub, if the Captain called a name from across the room, the crew member would snap to attention without hesitation, not out of fear, but because they knew the voice of someone who had led them well. His voice had become familiar, trusted, and unmistakable: the sound that led them through storms, called them to their posts, and reminded them of who they were. The Captain often smiled when it happened, proud of the bond they had built.

Life is full of distracting voices, many sounding sweet and accepting, but anything not from God will eventually ensnare and harm my soul, since I am far more vulnerable than I anticipated. It took secluding myself, walking to the edge of that pier in the blizzard, to finally hear His voice without distractions. By learning God's character through the Bible, I came to recognize His voice, because when He spoke, it was consistent with what I had read about Him. From that starting point, God and I built years of quiet mornings together, meeting in devotion, learning to hear His voice in a safe space. Over time, He began to lead me into more hectic places where I had to bring His voice with me. At first, it felt impossible, but little by little, it became my way of life. Now, I cannot imagine facing any situation without hearing Him clearly, no matter how stressful. He has become my only true guide, offering wisdom beyond what any human could give. After years of practice, I recognize His voice even among the noise of the world and my own thoughts. Often, what He asks of me defies logic, but it is not my job to judge His requests. I work for Him, not the other way around. He is a good Father, and His path, though difficult, leads directly to my true destiny.

John 10:5

CAPTAIN'S VOICE

The Captain carried his treasure with him everywhere the ship sailed. It was more than wealth; it was his key to truly living. If he had stayed on the family farm, working constantly just to scrape by, he would have died with aching hands and unfulfilled dreams. But now, after braving the sea and stumbling upon riches, he tasted a fullness of life he had never experienced before. With the weight of gold near him, his mind began to open. He found himself dreaming for the first time. What if he built a mansion, a kingdom, bought an island, or even the entire Caribbean? The freedom to imagine without fear changed him. No longer bound by survival, he stepped into big dreaming. The gold stirred something in him, a sense that anything was possible, and that the world might be greater than he had dared to believe.

It felt as if I had discovered a pair of wireless God-Phones, earbuds that turned any moment into a magical symphony from heaven. The music of God's voice filled my ears, bringing meaning, excitement, and purpose wherever I went. Driven by a deep hunger for Him, I began tuning in daily, learning what it meant to pray without ceasing. Instead of turning to worldly thinking or seeking answers from Artificial Intelligence, I paused and asked the Father, and He always offered wisdom that bore far more fruit than any human or machine could. I knew I was in God's presence when fear-based thinking disappeared and His voice encouraged me to dream big and see life through a good eye. I dreamed about which celebrities I would choose to partner with on my music invention and imagined my ideal house design and how I would use it for God's purposes once I had the resources to build it. I can gain knowledge from people, but true wisdom comes from being alone with Him. From the moment I wake, I keep my head in the clouds and my heart close to Papa, dreaming big alongside Him and embracing the greater plans He has for my life.

Psalm 37:4

BIG DREAMS

The ship halted en route to the Southern Spanish Main as the wind died down. The navigator turned to the captain with a smirk and asked if he would rather have the men struggle to row across the ocean or let the sea do the work. He pointed out a current he had tracked many times before, one mile westward, that would carry them swiftly south. The Captain trusted him, and sure enough, the ship began gliding forward with surprising ease. There was little wind, but the steady pull of the trade current moved them along like a gentle hand guiding their hull. The crew, used to sweat and toil, leaned back and let the sea carry them. In moments like these, it felt like the ocean itself was for them, not against them, and rest was well-received.

Walking with God in divine flow, resting in the palm of His plan each day, became the most peaceful way to live. God and I had traded kingdoms, and I watched in awe as He stewarded mine with incredible excellence. The less I forced things, the more progress unfolded. Connections for my music startup would appear at just the right time, and checks would arrive in the mail or other miraculous provision, covering my exact needs. This divine flow felt foolish to the world, but it was wise, like guiding a ship into a current that carries me exactly where I am meant to go. After tasting this way of life, I could see how exhausting it was for others to row against the current, straining for little gain. Stillness with Him was productive like floating weightless in a spaceship, where it seems nothing is happening, yet I was racing around the Earth at 17,000 miles per hour. In that stillness with Him, my mind, body, and soul found true strength and renewal.

Psalm 23:2-3

FLŌW ŌR RŌW

The Captain began to notice a shift among the crew. They had started smiling more, responding to his radical, spontaneous, and recurring generosity. Stories of his kindness spread quickly, and he liked it. He found joy in surprising his men with gifts from the treasure chest, watching their eyes light up with gratitude. Each time he gave, it stirred a memory from childhood, the joy of Christmas morning, sitting wide-eyed before his gifts. As a boy, his only task was to receive with thanks. Now, he stood on the other side of that moment, as the giver, and the joy was just as rich. Embracing this new identity, he made a decision. At their next port, he ordered the crew to paint over the old ship name, ***Fearmonger****. In its place, bold and gleaming, they wrote the new name:* ***Golden Tide****. It marked a turning point not just for the ship, but for the man who now steered it with open hands and a full heart.*

Charity Gayle is one of my favorite Christian music artists, so I was amazed when I received a random email from a friend, Dwan, inviting me to join the choir for her new album. It was being recorded just minutes from my house, even though she lives 600 miles away. After weeks of spiritual battles, this felt like such a sweet and timely gift from God. I had not sung in a choir since middle school, yet here I was about to sing on Charity's praise album, *Rejoice*. God had surprised me with a gift I had not worked for, and in that moment, I saw His generosity so clearly. I am still learning to stop striving and to trust that my Father knows my needs and provides in perfect timing. It is more blessed to give than to receive, so technically speaking, I bless God when I allow Him to give to me. His gifts fill me with the same wonder I felt as a child unwrapping a present, and all I want to do in return is overflow in generosity to others.

James 1:17

GOLDEN TIDE

As the Captain recalled additional joys of childhood Christmases, he chuckled at the memory of his English cousins who had moved to France, visiting Shaftesbury each year. Though they spoke no English anymore, they filled the house with laughter and energy, especially the youngest, a sweet little girl who charmed everyone with her playfulness. But when things didn't go her way, whether she missed out on the last pastry or was told they couldn't go to the beach, her tiny voice would erupt through the house in a fiery wail of ***"Ce n'est pas juste!"*** *meaning* ***"It's not fair."*** *The phrase echoed off the walls like a royal decree of injustice, exclaiming the unfair hardship of her life.*

I started noticing an unfair level of blessing the more I knew God. Before 2020, life often felt unfair. I lost jobs, fought with family and friends, and felt weighed down by chaos. Everything changed when I became a child of the King. Life shifted from unfair hardship to unfair blessing, and I began to wonder, *"Am I receiving too much favor?"* It's not fair being a son of the King, but it is an absolute blast. I've always loved building things with my hands as a designer, but after months of filming the music documentary with filmmakers, I prayed to connect with more *"maker-type"* people. One evening, driving to a friend's house for dinner, I had twenty minutes to spare. I spotted a sign that read *"Make Nashville,"* a co-working space for creators. Excited, I hit the brakes, pulled in, and knocked on the door. To my surprise, someone opened it and asked, *"You here for the tour?"* A biweekly tour was starting in just two minutes. I had arrived at the perfect moment. After the tour, I signed up for a membership, and it has been my favorite place in Nashville ever since. There, I build prototypes with wood, metal, and plastic, and create in community. God really does give unfair gifts to his kids that bless their hearts.

Romans 8:32

CE N'EST PAS JUSTE

As a boy, the Captain struggled to read and was labeled lazy, stupid, and useless. Desperate to survive school, he resorted to cheating on tests just to stay afloat, but at age 14, he was caught, beaten by his teacher, and expelled from the local grammar school. Years later, standing at the helm of a ship overflowing with treasure and camaraderie, he marveled at the irony. Back then, his creativity to survive brought punishment. Now, it felt like he and his crew were cheating life in a different way, breaking the rules, living richly, and yet blessing everyone around them. No one was being expelled from this ship. In fact, the chaos seemed to make them stronger. He smiled at the thought. What would his old teachers think if they could see him now, thriving in a life built not by following the rules, but by rewriting them?

The greatest life hack I have found is doing life with God. The crow's nest on His ship is higher, and He knows the wisest course through treacherous waters. Each morning, He often reveals what challenges lie ahead, preparing me perfectly for the day. One example among hundreds was Him nudging me that a friend would call at 10:00 a.m., upset and needing a safe space, and it happened, exactly as He said. His guidance, like that, helped me navigate the day with confidence, thinking less and resting more in His presence, ready to receive my friend's volatile heart. God's yoke is easy, and His burden is light. It is not about cutting corners but about embracing divine wisdom that leads me through every situation. In God's kingdom, success is not measured by how hard I work but by how fully I trust Him. When I lived apart from God, I hustled and strived to push my life forward, but all I gained was exhaustion and emptiness. When I let go and just do life with Him, He gifts me with the fullness of life that I could never have earned. Life with God is the sweetest gift.

John 10:10

CHEATING

With newfound free time, the Captain began exploring his creative side and developed a fondness for painting. Each time he stood before a blank canvas, a tender hush settled over him as he contemplated the endless possibilities it held. Would he flood it with vibrant pastels to capture the glory of a breathtaking sunset, or gently layer soft watercolors to reflect a lake surrounded by mountains, with a sailboat in the middle, leaving a beautiful wake? These quiet moments of imagination became sacred to him, a rare and gentle escape where the world slowed down and wonder took the helm.

Marty Solomon, founder of the BEMA Discipleship Podcast, is one of my favorite theologians. When he announced a book signing in Nashville, I signed up immediately, almost seeing him as larger than life. But on the day of the event, God spoke clearly to my heart, urging me to stay home. I had placed Marty on a pedestal, and the Lord invited me to spend that time with Him instead. Though it was hard, I surrendered my plans and chose to draw closer to God. Nine months later, out of the blue, I received an email from Marty himself inviting me to dinner. A coworker of his had mentioned me and suggested we connect when he came to Nashville. That dream came true in a far richer way than I ever imagined, as I shared a meaningful meal with Marty and his wife, so much sweeter than any book signing. God reminded me that when I put Him first, He exceeds my hopes. My life is His canvas, and the level to which I surrender determines the size of the masterpiece He paints.

Ephesians 3:20

CANVAS

Near the coast of the Southern Spanish Main, the crew stopped to explore the unfamiliar island of Aruba. As they docked, friendly indigenous tribesmen rushed out to greet them with warmth and hospitality. The crew was invited to share a meal, and a bond quickly formed. After eating, the tribe announced they were heading to a lagoon on the southwest side to fish and welcomed the pirates to join. There, the crew learned a new skill. The tribesmen carved four-pronged spears from slender branches and sharpened them to fine points, but before fishing, they placed the tips in the fire. At first, the Captain thought the flames would weaken the wood, but he soon discovered the opposite. The fire hardened the tips, strengthening them like metal and making them durable enough for repeated use. What seemed like destruction was actually preparation.

Growing up, I saw fasting as something for health fanatics, not something that mattered in my life. That changed when a mentor named Henry helped me see fasting through God's eyes. I began to understand biblical water fasting as a costly but beautiful sacrifice for deeper intimacy with Him. Like someone who saves for years to buy a dream car and gladly hands over the cash, fasting is a meaningful exchange. It invites me to weigh the value of God's will and the answers I seek in prayer. Is His intimacy and wisdom worth fasting for a day or two? What about a few weeks? The answer is yes because His ways are always better. Fasting sharpens my ability to hear His voice above the noise by removing distractions and creating space to focus entirely on Him. Just as the tribesmen hardened their spear tips in fire, strengthening them rather than weakening, fasting prepares me for what lies ahead, adding confidence that every step I take is in line with God's footprints. The devil's first temptation was with food, so it's no surprise that laying it down draws me closer to God. Some of my sweetest memories with Him have come when I was most hungry for His presence.

Matthew 6:16-18

SPEARFISHING

The natives enjoyed the company of the pirates so much that they invited them to stay on Aruba for a week. The islanders lived simply, but the pirates were amazed by their healing skills, especially when they eased Peg Leg's chronic leg pain. What began as a casual stop became a meaningful break from the high-energy holidays most pirates sought. Rather than chasing thrills, they camped in huts, told stories, and reflected on the journey since the captain discovered the treasure chest in Florida. The simplicity of life with the natives, focused on food, friendship, and thankfulness, offered a deeper joy than their usual revelry. As the week ended and they prepared to return to the ship, their hearts felt lighter. They were no longer rushing through life but cherishing it. The break had transformed them, helping them see the ship not as routine, but as a gift, one they would now step back onto with gratitude.

Before knowing God, I took high-dopamine vacations to escape my hard and boring life. I would chase as much fun as possible, only to crash back into reality a week later, depressed and let down by how difficult life felt. But recently, I've formed a new habit. Like Jesus, I began withdrawing to desolate places in nature to spend time with the Father. As an avid explorer, I now spend all the free time I can alone in the wilderness, far from any human in sight. Life out there is pure and simple. Stripped down, all I really need is food, friends, and God. The first couple of days camping without my phone are uncomfortable, as I resist the urge to chase instant gratification. But then my mind settles, and I become present, soaking in the beauty around me. Deprived of the usual dopamine rushes, I realize that technology is a major contributor to my anxieties, and I grow deeply grateful for the simple things. God fills the empty space I create, overflowing my soul with His presence. I return home refreshed, renewed by His Spirit, and thankful for every little thing.

Psalm 23:2-3

ISLAND VACATION

As the pirates prepared to say goodbye, they offered parting gifts to the locals, who in return surprised the crew with pet monkeys in cages and three large barrels of their finest salt from nearby salt flats. Each barrel was worth quite a bit, and though the villagers had little to spare and might never see the crew again, they gave generously. The gesture stirred something deep in the captain's heart, reminding him of his childhood in England. His grandparents lived far off in Whitby, too ill to visit often, but every year without fail, a birthday package would arrive from his grandfather. His heart would pound with expectation. Was it a tin of sweets, a set of carved animals, or a wooden toy ship? The mystery often kept him awake at night, his imagination dancing with joy. Now, watching the barrels of salt being hoisted aboard, the Captain felt that same wonder in receiving such a precious gift.

As the deadline for a hefty patent fee for my music invention approached, I found myself without the funds to cover it. Instead of focusing solely on my financial need, God nudged me to first seek His kingdom. He prompted me to gather a group of Nashville friends for a weekend trip to Randy's house church in Florida, aiming to spark hunger for spiritual revival in Nashville. With the payment due the Monday after our return and no time to pitch to investors, I spent the week organizing schedules for this unexpected God-led journey. After a 12-hour drive to the gathering on Friday evening, I received a random text from someone out of state whom I had never pitched to. They asked about my patent fee and said they felt led by God to give me the exact amount needed. Miraculously, they provided the funds just two days before the deadline. Grateful for His provision, I began documenting His goodness in my journal, a spiritual savings account reminding me of His unwavering faithfulness. Now I praise Him in advance, and eagerly check my spiritual mailbox daily, ready to receive His blessings.

Hebrews 11:1

SPECIAL DELIVERY

Word of the Captain's generosity and excellent crew spread across the seas. Eager sailors from many ports approached him, asking, ***"Captain, can we join your crew?"*** *His heart longed to say yes, but the ship was full, and he had to turn them away. Eventually, he realized he needed a second ship, though he did not feel ready. The idea of doubling his responsibilities felt crushing. But then the vision became clear. He had the treasure. He had people desperate to join something meaningful. All that was missing was his yes. So he gave it. The next ship he encountered, he would purchase, not for status but to make space for those seeking purpose. And he already knew who would captain it, his faithful peg-legged helmsman. It would not be easy, but deep down, he believed the perfect ship would find him when the time was right.*

After returning from Florida, I felt so inspired by Randy's gathering that I thought it was time to launch something similar in Nashville. But when I asked God, He threw me a curveball. Even though I was already chest-deep in developing my music invention, God prompted me to also write a book of Kingdom parables and testimonies from my journal. The timing felt terrible and impossible, given my full startup workload and my struggle with dyslexia. I was sure now was the time to bring my music product to market, especially with the patent status. How could I possibly write a book on top of that? And who would want to read a book written by someone who struggles with reading, doesn't like writing, and doesn't even enjoy books? But God reminded me that His power is made perfect in weakness. The only reason people should love this book is because of His stories, not my competence. This book was to make God more famous. I said yes, with no idea where to begin, but ready for His dream to unfold. My Heavenly Father authored a bestselling book, and now I guess it was time for His son to follow in His footsteps.

Proverbs 3:5-6

FLEET

While daydreaming on the quarterdeck about the mighty fleet he hoped to build, the captain glanced down and was shocked to notice a snail resting on the railing beside his hand. He blinked in surprise. Where had it emerged from? Snails are the slowest little creatures, yet they have a strange magic about them, appearing suddenly, as if out of thin air. He never saw it coming, yet here it was, silently arriving without a trace. Just as he pondered the mystery, a cry rang out from above. "Land ho!" shouted the lookout from the crow's nest, breaking the spell as the hazy outline of the Southern Spanish Main emerged on the horizon.

I complained again, telling God I'd need at least a hundred parables to make a book people would actually want to buy. I was sure I only had about thirty parables in my journal, but He said, *"Count them."* To my shock, I found over 130 already recorded. Then I remembered a moment from three years earlier when Randy's wife, Tammy, prophesied that I'd write a book. I had laughed it off, knowing my dyslexia and complete lack of desire to write. Yet during my devotional time, God had been quietly fulfilling that prophecy. What I thought was just journaling parables to better understand His character turned out to be the weaving of an entire book meant to bless the world. Progress had snuck up on me like a snail, surprising everyone, including myself. As an artist, I was most excited to illustrate the book myself, but God surprised me by asking me to hire my friend Stephen instead, to share the kingdom's wealth. This frustrated me, but I agreed. When we completed our first rough draft with just 25 illustrated parables, people were brought to tears and said they'd buy cases. God then led me to wrap all 100 parables into a pirate adventure, creating a melody that made the message sing, a spoonful of sugar that helped the medicine go down, turning deep spiritual truths into a fun treasure hunt rather than a heavy-handed lecture.

Habakkuk 2:3

MAGIC SNAIL

There they were, the shimmering peaks of the Santa Marta coast rising like a promise on the horizon. But just as hope stirred, the wind vanished and the currents stilled, leaving the ***Golden Tide*** *motionless. With no other choice, the crew lowered the longboats and began the grueling task of rowing, towing their ship inch by inch. The sun beat down, sweat stung their eyes, and their muscles ached with every pull. Facing backward as they rowed, they could not see the mountains ahead, only the endless sea behind, which made progress feel like a guess. Doubts crept in.* ***What if they never arrived? What if the cliffs were too steep to climb? What if it wasn't worth the effort?*** *But none of that mattered now. Their only task was simple: row together in unison.*

As I scrambled to create materials to impress potential partners with my music invention, I kept hitting walls and falling behind. Then God asked me to do something that made no sense: fast for three days while camping in the Mountains. God's ways are higher, so I said yes. I went into the wilderness, fully aware I'd look like a fool if He didn't come through in response to my obedience. Those three days were transformative. God taught me to lock eyes with Him through the urgency, staying present each day, focusing on reaching the next mountain range, not stressing over what was beyond it, just enjoying Him. Why waste energy fretting over what's beyond the horizon of today or even after death when God invites me to trust Him in the simple rowing of daily life? Whatever lies beyond today or even this life will be amazing as long as He's by my side. When I returned refreshed from camping, God gave me a brilliant business idea: turn my pitch deck into a comic book. I finished it in record time, and it sparked a curiosity that no other presentation could. While I rested with God, He worked in ways I couldn't have planned, opening doors and providing solutions better than I had imagined.

Matthew 6:34

SHIP TŌW

The quartermaster's son was chasing the ship's dog across the deck when he accidentally collided with the navigator, sending the precious spyglass flying. It hit the wood and shattered into pieces across the deck. The spyglass was the most expensive and essential tool on board, used to scout land, ports, and distant ships. Anger and panic rose in the captain's chest as he imagined sailing blind, vulnerable, and lost. He began to yell at the boy. But then he paused. This was his old mindset, rooted in scarcity and fear. He remembered who he was, not poor or desperate, but the richest man in the region, and could replace the spyglass. With a deep breath, he calmed himself, apologized to the boy, and assured them both that at the next port, they would buy the finest spyglass available. There was nothing to fear.

During that camping trip, my business life felt shattered. I felt behind on the startup, behind on the book, and spending time camping instead of being "productive" crushed me at first. The enemy attacked my mind with fearful thoughts: *God won't come through this time. If I don't get the materials prepped, the meetings will flop, the funding will fall through, I'll go hungry, and my life will collapse. I'm being lazy*. But God's perfect love casts out fear, and all those voices were simply lies. God reminded me that I was walking on water, something that made no sense to my old self. But as a son of the King, I could lock eyes with my Father in trust. It was tempting to bypass God's ways. To try to gain power, wealth, and influence quickly through manipulation, idolatry, or disobedience. But God called me to stay rooted in His way, even through the pain. That's the only path to true, lasting prosperity. God showed me that if losing anything could destroy me, it was an idol. Building my startup had begun to overshadow my hunger for Him. So in that broken place in the wilderness, I returned my heart to God, and He filled every part.

1 John 4:18

SPYGLASS

A newer sailor they had picked up in Tortuga stood in stunned silence, his jaw hanging open at the Captain's calm response to the shattered spyglass. He knelt beside the quartermaster's son and shared his own story, explaining how on his last ship, he had once slipped and dropped a box of food overboard. For that mistake, his former captain ordered twenty lashes and denied him food for a week. He pulled up his shirt to reveal the thick scars crisscrossing his back, and the boy gasped. The sailor shook his head in disbelief, imagining how that same brutal captain would have had him keelhauled or even executed for destroying something as important as a spyglass. Yet here on the ***Golden Tide****, the Captain had simply forgiven the mistake and promised to buy a finer replacement at the next port. The boy looked down, realizing just how fortunate he was to serve under a captain who led with mercy rather than fear.*

In July 2021, I accidentally dropped my beloved Teenage Engineering OP-Z music sequencer, breaking its Bluetooth and leaving it unable to connect to my phone to fine-tune settings. I tried more than twenty fixes and even contacted support, only to be told I would need to spend six hundred dollars on a replacement. Over four years later, I desperately needed the Bluetooth for a demo of my music invention. For the first time, I prayed about it, and to my amazement, it connected perfectly on the first try. God fixed what had seemed unfixable, right on time. My life has transformed under His care. I used to be a slave to work, exhausted and stressed, surrounded by people who treated me with manipulation and pressure, just as I had come to expect from the world's captains. But under the Good Shepherd, I am daily stunned by His kindness. It feels as if blessings spill into my life simply because I stay close to Him, and I am flourishing in ways I never imagined.

Psalm 23:6

BAD CAPTAIN

As the men painstakingly rowed, Peg Leg's voice rang out across the waves, lifting their spirits with another story from the priest. He spoke of a boy named Joseph, a favorite of his father and chosen by God for greatness, yet hated by his brothers and thrown into a pit before being sold into slavery. But Joseph did not give up. He worked so hard for his master that he rose through the ranks. Then came betrayal, his master's wife falsely accused him, and Joseph was thrown into prison. Still, he did not give up. He served with joy even in chains, and in time, God lifted him from the prison floor to the palace throne, making him second-in-command to the most powerful king in the world. Peg Leg turned to the men and shouted above the crashing oars, to keep rowing through the pain, and like Joseph, glory waits on the other side. With renewed strength, the men towed ***Golden Tide*** *towards the shimmering shore.*

During my hardest seasons, millionaires approached me, saying they wanted what I had. Though my life felt painful and chaotic, they saw the joy and peace within me. They couldn't understand how I was content with only my basic needs met, while they felt empty despite every luxury. From the world's view, following God makes little sense. Christians often lose what they value most and face rejection, attacks, or even death for their faith. Yet what they gain is worth far more than anything lost. Even on my worst days, I'm grateful simply to be alive and serving Him. How tempting it must have been for Joseph to take control, break out of prison, and risk derailing God's plan. Instead, he chose obedience over control, trusting God's provision and power even in prison. He simply thanked God in advance for meeting his needs and setting him free. Now, with my own catalogue of God's faithfulness and miracles, I remind myself in stretching moments: *"Stop worrying and praise God for the gift that's already on the way. His story is good."*

Genesis 50:19-21

PRISŌN

The men finally towed the ship close enough to drop anchor and take the longboats ashore, their arms aching but spirits high. As they waded into the warm shallows beneath the Santa Marta mountains, something caught their eyes: thousands of oysters. The Captain, grinning ear to ear, knelt down and picked up his first oyster in months. With a twinkle in his eye, he quoted Shakespeare, ***"Why then, the world's mine oyster, which I with sword will open."*** *The crew roared with laughter as the captain slurped it down, savoring the tasty reward after a long journey.*

The Bible verse *"Your Heavenly Father knows what you need before you ask"* used to frustrate me. It felt like a cruel guessing game. Why ask for anything if He already knew? But then Jamie Winship offered a new perspective: if my Father in heaven already knows what I need, shouldn't I start by asking Him what I actually need and then pray for that? This world is not my oyster; it's my Father's, and He knows exactly what I need to thrive. The first time I prayed that way, I thought I needed $300 to cover my credit card, but when I asked God what I needed, He said $600. Sure enough, $600 was due the next day. God told me to call a specific friend for help, but before calling, He asked me to plan a celebration in advance as an act of faith. It felt strange to prepare a celebration before making the call, but I chose to step out in trust and decided I'd visit a favorite restaurant that evening. It was humbling, as a 27-year-old man, to ask my friend for help. But to my surprise, they were overjoyed to give. They told me God had been teaching them about radical generosity and had put me on their heart that very morning. They were even more excited to give than I was to receive. Since then, I've trusted God to define my needs, and He has provided in ways that continue to leave me in awe.

Matthew 6:8

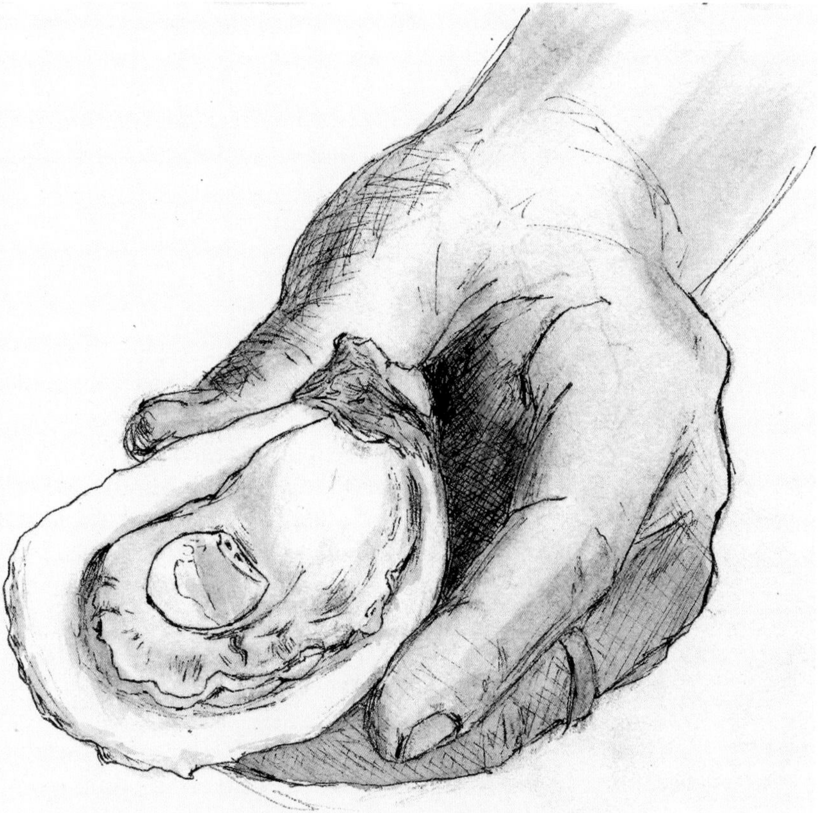

MY FATHER'S OYSTER

As the sun dipped toward the horizon, the crew gathered on the beach to collect firewood and prepare camp, chopping down trees before darkness fell. But first, they had to scrape the rust from their axes and sharpen the edges, knowing full well that a dull blade was more dangerous than a sharp one. A dull edge required brute force to cut, increasing the chance of injury, while a sharp blade sliced clean with minimal effort. As the Captain honed his axe, he drifted into a daydream of a mythical axe so finely crafted it never dulled, able to slice through rock as easily as driftwood. He smiled at the thought, knowing even his great wealth could not buy such a thing. With their blades gleaming once more, the crew rose to their feet and marched into the woods to claim what the land had to offer.

Leading up to Christmas, I was broke. I had paid lawyer fees to finalize my patent, filmed expensive promo videos for my music invention, and printed rough drafts of my book to ship nationwide for feedback. I had no money left to fly home for Christmas. When I asked God what to do, He made it clear that He wanted me in Michigan to love my family. So I prayed, *"Then please provide the funds."* Weeks passed, and ten days before Christmas, I pleaded again. But God said, *"I want you to be there. Trust me. Buy the flight on credit, and I'll provide."* So, using what I jokingly called a "God-it card", I told my mentor on a call that I would purchase the flight in obedience without a clue how I'd pay it back. Seconds after that call ended, my friend Brian randomly phoned to offer me a cash job helping his son drive from Nashville to Alaska starting New Year's Day, paying more than four times the cost of the flight. God's favor felt like a blade slicing through every obstacle. When I say yes to Him, no task is too daunting. All I have to do is trust His support and watch Him carve a path with ease.

2 Corinthians 10:17

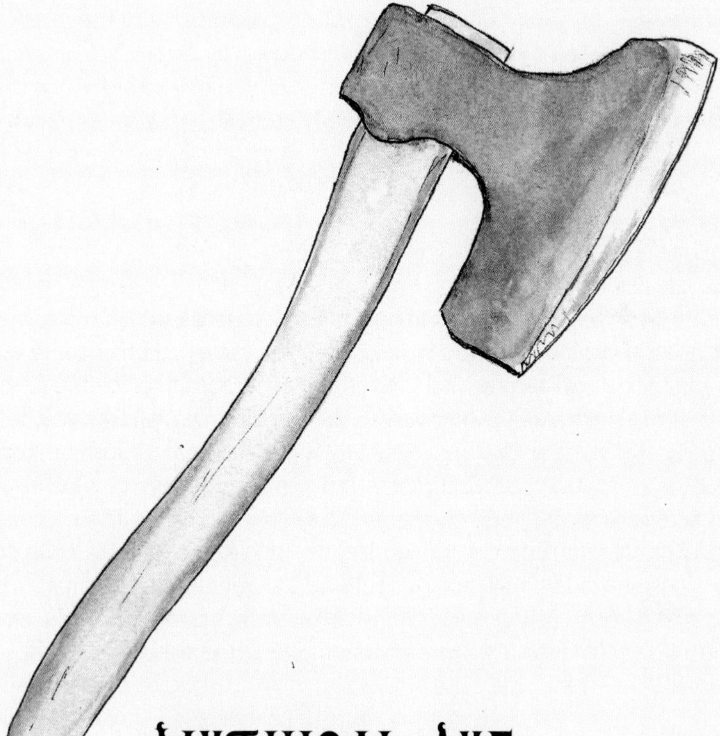

MYTHICAL AXE

While chopping trees for firewood, the Captain paused to admire the towering forest that blanketed the mountains. He marveled at the sheer number of trees and called out to his ship craftsman, asking why such an abundance of timber was not used to build ships. The craftsman pointed to several fallen trees scattered through the woods and gave an unexpected answer. These trees, though tall and impressive, had grown up in a windless region, which also explained why the crew had to row the ship into shore. This part of the Spanish Main rarely saw strong winds, so the trees never developed the strength needed to withstand pressure. Without resistance during their growth, they shot up too quickly, growing weak and unstable. In time, each of them collapses under its own weight. So they were useless for shipbuilding. A ship built from their wood might look strong, but the first real storm would shatter it into pieces.

Around New Year's Day, Brian's son Calvin and I set off from Nashville, eager to drive to Alaska and take in the stunning scenery of the northwest. All felt like an adventure until we reached Vancouver and began to understand why so few people tackle the Alaska highway in winter. The road ahead was desolate, with stretches of hundreds of miles between gas stops or buildings. People have frozen to death there in blizzards, stranded without help, with grizzlies lurking in the forests. The forecast showed temperatures dropping to -40 in the region. Our truck was big but unprepared: no winter tires, no chains, no stockpile of food. Fear crept in as we realized bad weather could add a week to our journey. We prayed, asking if God wanted us to continue. He answered yes. Miraculously, as we drove, temperatures rose nearly 70 degrees, reaching 30 degrees Fahrenheit, unheard of for January. God kept us safe the entire way. The sun shone only from 10:00 to 3:00, so much of our drive was in darkness, but we praised God through the dark. He was shaping me to stand strong in life's storms.

Romans 5:3

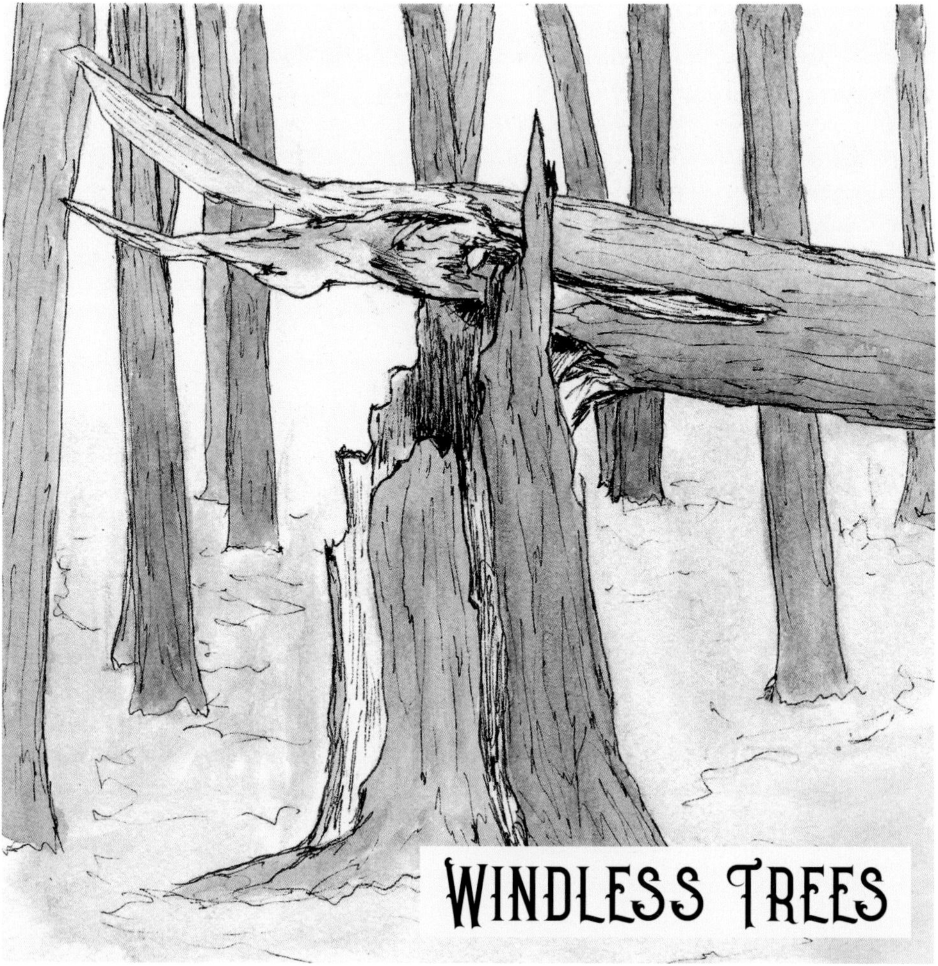
WINDLESS TREES

After a hearty feast, the crew gathered around the crackling fire. Peg Leg launched into heroic tales, his voice rising and falling with dramatic flair as the others listened wide-eyed. The Captain let the moment wash over him. He took in the tree-covered mountains around their hidden cove, the cool sand beneath his feet, and the mirror-still sea cradling his anchored ship. Above it all, a full moon shone impossibly bright, ruling the night sky with silver light like the star of its own grand play. The moon was a pale ghost in daylight, easily ignored, yet here it commanded every gaze in its radiance. The Captain felt a deep swell of gratitude, counting himself the luckiest man alive to roam the mysterious corners of this beautiful world while sharing these nights with the loyal mates who called him captain.

Driving through the Yukon for endless hours in the pitch-black winter darkness felt strange, but the shadows were filled with the soft glow of moonlight. God showed me something powerful in that moment in realizing the moon had no light of its own.. As His son, my job is not to create my own light but to reflect His, just like the moon reflects the sun. When I keep my eyes on Him, I paint the world with light, but the moment I look away, my light fades. And this world is desperate for light. Again, I am no one special. All I did was begin talking with God. I asked Him what He wanted me to know and to do. God is not a wishing well for my desires. But, for example, when He asked me to move to Nashville and I needed a car, I stepped forward in faith, trusting He would provide, and He did. Success in God's eyes is simple: ask for His wisdom, then obey. When I sail with Him, His light shines through, and people are drawn to the glow. **The only thing that shines brighter than this is a whole community of people doing it together as a crew.**

Philippians 2:15

MOONLIGHT

...AND CELEBRATES WITH HIS MATES.

What's next?

Acts 2:46–47

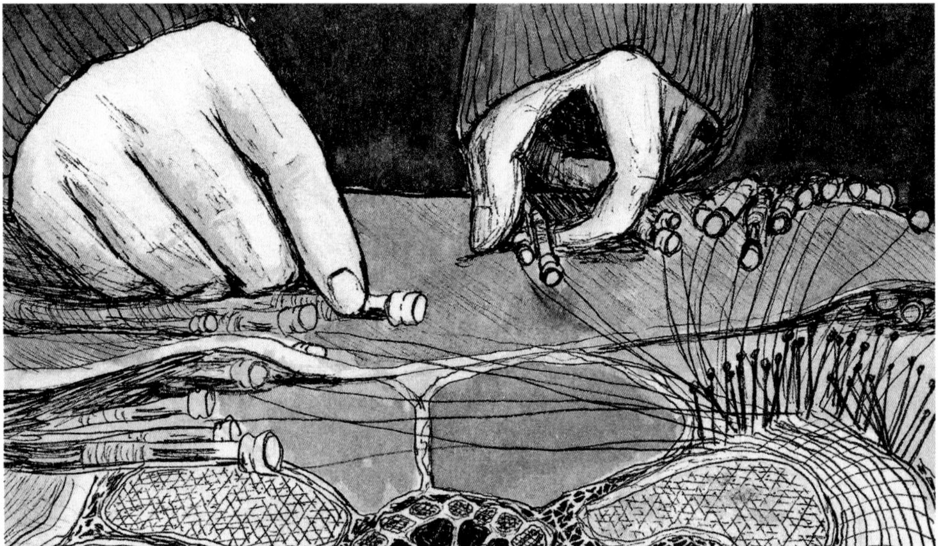
MASS PRŌDUCTIŌN

As the Captain gazed into the bonfire flames, his mind drifted back to childhood and the ache of missing his aunt, uncle, and cousins, loved ones he rarely saw again after they left for France in search of work. His Uncle had been a skilled craftsman, a master of the delicate art of making decorative fabric lace by hand. For generations, handmade lace was considered an exquisite treasure, requiring years of training to perfect and costing a fortune to own. But the world changed swiftly. New machines allowed factories to mass-produce lace at a fraction of the cost, prioritizing profit over quality. The machine-made lace was far inferior, and worse, it robbed thousands of artisans of their livelihoods almost overnight. The Captain's relatives were among those devastated by this harsh turn of fortune, forced to abandon their country to survive. The Captain felt the weight of their lost craftsmanship and way of life, both sacrificed for cheaper goods and greater gain.

As I deepened my relationship with God, I began feeling a strange emptiness every Sunday at most church services, surrounded by hundreds of people watching a pastor on an elevated stage. Though the sermons were sometimes inspiring, they felt like quick bites meant to keep attendees returning, as if the goal were to mass-produce Christians in a factory building a brand with minimal care rather than truly transforming lives. I want to honor the sincere hearts of believers and leaders in the Western corporate church model, even when they're unaware or feeling stuck, yet I can't shake the longing for the kind of living, breathing community Jesus envisioned. Western churches often focus on larger stages and growing attendance, but this growth can produce shallow conversions and miss the depth that Jesus modeled. His ministry was intimate. He chose twelve disciples rather than twelve hundred, creating space for real, personal growth without charging them anything. If even Jesus, the King of the universe, chose a small circle of friends, perhaps I am called to embrace slow, intentional discipleship where genuine care and deep investment matter far more than numbers.

John 10:14-15

STRANGE SOUND

The morning after the bonfire, the Captain heard a scraping sound as he passed the hammock of a young boy in the crew. Curious, he drew closer and saw the boy sharpening a blade. Yet the knife was hardly a blade at all, worn down to a thin nub from nonstop grinding. The boy's hands trembled as he worked, fearful of looming battles and unsure how he would defend himself. The Captain chuckled softly, startling him, then placed a reassuring hand on his shoulder. He promised there was nothing to fear, for the crew would teach him to fight so he could stand with confidence among comrades.

For many Americans, specifically Gen Z, life is marked by the opposite of the fruits of the Spirit, with an average of nine hours of screen time daily, soaring rates of depression (42%), anxiety (60%), loneliness (73%), and impatient attention spans of just eight seconds. People are starving for genuine connection, yet can rarely find anyone willing to truly sit with them. Meanwhile, the corporate-branded Western church often promises community, yet the fruit of this mass-production model leaves loads of people spiritually empty. The Western church itself isn't the enemy; real spiritual forces are at work, tempting it toward fear, division, and separation. Every year, over a million young people walk away from the church, the largest generational shift away from faith in American history, leaving families heartbroken and searching for answers. This is not God's fault; He has not changed. Unchurched people long for proof that God cares about their real emotional and mental struggles. Yet instead of offering presence and support, many corporate churches hold genuine relationships hostage, demanding volunteering and tithing as though connection must be earned. Jesus showed a better way, laying down His life to walk alongside people. Sunday services can feel like endlessly sharpening blades without ever practically using them, wearing souls down to nubs. I enjoy praising God with friends at Sunday services, but if that were my only spiritual act during the week, most of my God stories in this book would have never happened.

Hebrews 10:24-25

LOST NAVIGATOR

The crew sailed west and docked at Cartagena, where the Captain began recruiting for their future ship. A man claiming to be a master navigator with 20 years of experience offered his services, provided the pay matched his lofty standards. Something felt off, so the Captain pressed him. The truth soon surfaced: the man had never navigated a ship in his life, only talked about it with a friend who had. The Captain laughed, seeing his younger self, bored, arrogant, and blind to ambition's harm, reflected in the pretender. Knowing such inexperience could endanger the crew, he refused to hire him as navigator but offered a start as a swabbie. Enraged that his bluff had been exposed, the man stormed off, his dreams of easy power dashed against the rocks of truth.

Why would God entrust kingdom work to people whose entire *"training"* consists of attending 200 sermons without apprenticeship or authentic experience? The Western corporate-branded church model feels like a side dish of potatoes. Sides can complement a meal, but when they become the entire meal over and over, people grow sick, like sailors with scurvy. As Tom Wadsworth explains, much church pain stems from an overemphasis on vertical edification; most Western gatherings point only upward to God. Attendees walk in to sing, sit facing a stage to hear a pastor's revelations, take communion in silent devotion, then exit so the next crowd can have the same isolated spiritual experience. This leaves people empty and unsupported, needing to self-edify apart from services. It often breeds a model of self-help sermons, entertainment-driven praise, social club factions, brand-building, neglect of the poor, celebrity culture, and safety at all costs. Yet there is great hope for the Western church, as a coming movement will radically deepen what it means to be a disciple of Jesus, bringing a richer, fuller expression of faith. To grow a healthy, thriving church, I believe the protein-rich main course should return to center stage, and the potato side dish take its rightful place. Genuine horizontal edification builds people up like strong, interlocking bricks in a living wall.

James 1:22

WIN WITHOUT FIGHTING

It became harder for the Captain to relate to other crews who lived only to steal, leaving wakes of pain. His own crew had found a better way, exploring the world without harming a soul. He longed for others to see this and come aboard. Since finding treasure, his crew moved with freedom and joy, unlike the hardened faces of other crews, carrying misery like heavy chains. The Captain knew arguing with them would change nothing. He chose instead to focus on building the finest fleet on the seas. He poured his heart into making his sailors strong, free, and joyful, so that when others looked on, they would hunger for a life richer than gold and leave their hurtful ways behind.

Horizontal edification is not a new idea but a return to what the church practiced for its first three hundred years, gathering in homes through discipleship. This was the greatest proportional explosion of Christianity in history, nearly overtaking the Roman Empire through genuine, fruitful community. Scripture shows believers meeting in homes, sharing meals, and building one another up in love. Things shifted when Constantine legalized Christianity in 313 A.D., funding basilicas patterned after temples and theaters, with priests on stages before rows of passive attendees. That pattern birthed what are now called church services, moving the focus from intimate feasts to formal events. Communion narrowed from a shared table of bread and wine into a quiet altar ritual. For nearly two millennia, the temple style has shaped much of church life, often sidelining the personal discipleship Jesus modeled. God designed the tabernacle and temple for His presence, yet from the beginning desired to dwell directly with His people. Jesus foretold the destruction of the Jerusalem temple and taught that God would make His home in human hearts. In the New Testament, church meant gatherings of Spirit filled believers on mission together, not buildings. I believe if even 100 people in one city rose daily to hear God and obey, any city could be transformed. How can Christians recover true horizontal edification, nurture maturity, and see faith flourish more?

1 Corinthians 6:19

LAZY SHEPHERD

The Captain loved his new life of adventure fueled by treasure, but he often reflected on the stark contrast of his hardest year as a boy in Shaftesbury. One planting season, on a day so hot even the trees seemed to droop, his father set the grain seeds out to sow. Their neighbor, a careless shepherd, had fallen asleep, letting one hundred sheep loose into the grain fields. The boy's father spent the entire day chasing the neighbor's animals, trying to help, while his pile of precious seeds sat forgotten under the scalding sun. By evening, the seeds were spoiled, and the family lost the entire crop. The year that followed was marked by hunger and hardship, all because his father had abandoned the work that was his to do. If his father had simply sown the seed, they would have reaped a harvest.

Just as grain seeds left in a pile spoil in the sun, I have realized that gathering large numbers of believers into a single building week after week can lead to stagnation in spiritual maturity. The seeds were never meant to be stored in heaps; they were meant to be scattered and planted to bear fruit that spreads across the land. As seen in the early church, when believers disperse like seeds throughout neighborhoods, meeting in homes, sharing meals, and building one another up, they create fertile ground for authentic growth. Harvest does not come from centralizing saints but from sowing them. The fullest fruit emerges when believers meet regularly in homes, sharing full meals where everyone is an equal saint and fellow disciple of Jesus. In these horizontally edifying feasts, anyone can speak and be heard, creating an environment of true connection and shared growth. Practicing communion becomes part of the meal, using real bread and wine to remember the blessings of Jesus's sacrifice. This biblical model is beautifully simple, economically sustainable without facilities or salaries, socially rich in camaraderie, deeply personal in relationships, and universally repeatable by any follower of Christ. These feasts nourish individuals and offer the world a taste of His goodness.

Matthew 13:23

STŌP & HELP

As the crew prepared to leave Cartagena, the Captain worked on raising the sails. In a moment of overexertion at the ropes, he threw out his back. The ship's surgeon stood at a loss, unable to offer relief. The Captain, unable to stand from the pain, was carried to his bed, and the mission came to a halt. The crew knew nothing mattered until their Captain was restored. As he lay in agony, they gathered to consider how to help. Peg Leg recalled the natives of Aruba who had once eased his leg pain with their remedies. Without delay, they turned the ship and sailed three days to Aruba with the Captain groaning in pain. The islanders welcomed them with joy, but grief at the Captain's suffering. With skilled hands, they worked over him, and within minutes of care, the pain vanished. He laughed at the speedy healing, and the crew marveled at the kindness and wisdom of their native friends.

In the early church, gathering regularly for meals in homes functioned as a practice ground for love, caring for one another, and building each other up just as God builds up. Spiritual gifts were never meant to be kept silent in a service but shared freely, with everyone offering their gifts and recognizing them in others. Home Gatherings were really the ideal time to exercise and help others grow in gifts like prophecy, teaching, shepherding, evangelism, and apostleship because of the intimate environment. These meetings became rich with teaching and encouragement, comforting one another, forgiving, practicing hospitality, praising God, and meeting needs with patience and kindness. Love was the essential mandate of each gathering, truly living out the way of Christ. The church was called a body for a reason. Just as the Captain stopped everything when his back cried out in pain, so too the early church would halt and care for any member who was hurting. As gatherings deepened in intimacy, people began to feel like family, united as one body that would not advance until every part was restored.

1 Corinthians 12:26

STURDY SHIP

With the Captain's back healed, the crew set sail for Port Royal to gather more hands for the second ship. As they journeyed, the ship's craftsman taught the Captain about the unique construction of the **Golden Tide**, *showing him what to seek in a future vessel. The Captain marveled at the lower decks, where each wooden board leaned on and supported the next. Every plank was essential to keep the ship afloat, and if even one were missing or cracked, the entire vessel could be lost.* **Golden Tide** *was in exceptional condition, a rare ship and likely one of the strongest of its time, leaving the Captain to wonder how he could ever find another like it without stealing, as such sturdy vessels were rarely sold. Yet he felt confident the right ship would come at the right time.*

I believe the church is meant to function like a well-built ship, each plank adding unique strength to make the vessel unsinkable, rather than placing all the weight on a single voice. Yet the Western corporate model often relies on one-sided sermons delivered through microphones, like a ship with one strong board and many weak ones. In my experience, dialogue produces far more fruit than monologue. Jesus offered His greatest lessons in response to questions, and notably, the New Testament never uses the word *"sermon."* Biblical preaching most often occurred in evangelistic settings, not in house gatherings. Early believers met intimately in homes, fostering mutual encouragement, interactive teaching, and shared testimony, something nearly impossible in a building designed for a thousand silent listeners. Real growth happens where everyone's gifts are welcomed, affirmed, and exercised. Imagine if elders focused less on managing stages and more on protecting these small, Spirit-led spaces where believers reflect on Scripture together and recognize the Holy Spirit in one another. This shared-responsibility model of house church could raise up countless new leaders, strengthen the body, and remove the financial burden of ministry salaries and costly facilities. With everyone engaged in the marketplace, wealth could be generated to care for the needy and shine light into the world.

Ephesians 4:16

160 MILES

The lookout spotted a dot on the sea horizon. With no land ahead, the crew watched as it became a skiff with one man rowing furiously. The Captain ordered the anchor dropped. Sunburned, dehydrated, and starving but grinning, the man demanded to be hoisted aboard. Between gulps of water, he shared that he had rowed 160 miles over ten days from Jamaica, chasing the legend of the ***Golden Tide.*** *He had heard whispers of a crew living free and rich without stealing and was determined to find them. With no map and only hope, he risked everything, rowing into the unknown. The Captain was moved by his courage and offered him a place on the ship. His spirit was rare, a pirate willing to lose everything not for treasure, but for the chance to be part of something greater than gold.*

I used to doubt the early church's fruit and argue it wouldn't work today until I experienced it lived out firsthand at Randy's home church in Florida. Randy and his wife, Tammy, moved their family to Florida for his work in urban revitalization. Randy met a college student named Daniel, and through relationship, discipled and fathered him for years, helping him move from an orphan-hearted mindset into sonship. As Daniel slowly grew in this place of rest, the fruit multiplied. Randy and Tammy then opened up their home to mentor and disciple young adults into their true identity in Christ. After a year of gradual growth around meals and the presence of God, the group began to multiply, continuing to gather and meet each other's needs. The fruit in their lives was so undeniably visible in all of them that it stirred curiosity in others they met in public, who wanted to find the same treasure. The hungry rowed from miles away through the doors like the man in the skiff, and that's how their home gathering began to grow in what's now known as *KOH HAUS*.

Matthew 13:45-46

CAPTAIN'S COVENANT

Before the man from the skiff could join, he stood before the Captain to speak the covenant binding all who sailed with the ***Golden Tide.*** *The wind tugged at his tattered clothes as he faced the crew, ready to pledge his loyalty and begin anew. The sea seemed to hush as the Captain stepped forward and spoke loud and clear:* ***"Under the banner of the Golden Tide: Ye have the right to live in peace. No blade nor storm may claim what sails beneath her. Fear holds no place aboard this crew. Trust the course, and be guarded to the grave. What ye need shall be given: unseen, unearned, never late. If peril finds ye, the Captain shall rise in your name, and the sea itself shall bear witness. Do ye understand the rights of those who sail beneath the Golden Tide? And havin' heard them, do ye now swear to voyage by bold trust, not fear, to bear treasure not for takin', but for givin'?"*** *"AYE AYE!" cried the new pirate, grinning as he embraced the crew.*

Americans are steeped in legal rights, which can blur the lines between what God allows and what the government permits. I often found myself asking: *What rights do I truly have in God's Kingdom?* Over time, the major terms of joining God's ship became clear: 1. **The right to remain in peace** - No force can override the name of Jesus, who reigns supreme. 2. **Freedom from fear** - Perfect love casts out fear. When I stand in faith, no weapon formed against me shall prosper. 3. **The right to divine provision** - My Father knows what I need and provides in His perfect timing, out of His abundance. 4. **Heavenly legal representation** - Jesus Christ is my advocate before the highest court of heaven. By His blood, I am redeemed, justified, and have full access to God's throne. These aren't mere hopes; they're spiritual rights, sealed by covenant. Aboard God's ship, I carry these truths into peace and into battle, reminded that I am a citizen of Heaven, and the Captain always keeps His word.

Hosea 2:19-20

Who's Gonna Weigh Anchor

As the crew prepared to continue their journey back to Port Royal, it was time to weigh anchor. The pirates slid bars into the capstan and pushed in a circle with steady strength to turn the drum and haul up the heavy anchor line from the depths. The work was grueling under the sun, yet no one shrank from it. On many ships, this task was dreaded and given to the lowest hands as punishment, but on the **Golden Tide**, *the crew eagerly raised their hands, each man eager to join in and claim his part in the work. The new sailor watched, astonished by their joy and unity. In that moment, he knew for certain the rumors were true: the grass truly was greener on the* **Golden Tide**, *and he had made the best choice of his life.*

Weighing anchor is like carrying crosses in the spiritual world, where someone must be willing to bear them. Who is going to carry the crosses? True discipleship is not impossible, but it requires laying down one's life for others and walking closely together. The time for pointing fingers is over; now is the time to carry the cross and bring God's kingdom to earth through open ears and obedience to His voice. Mass-producing believers may seem easier at first, but it cannot replace real discipleship. Jesus' way often feels slow and wasteful in the short term, yet it bears exponential fruit over time, bringing true revival. (A great resource for launching house churches is ***LK10.com***.) God and I practice what I call kingdom swaps: I entrust Him with my kingdom while He entrusts me with His. I lay myself down and obey His leading, bringing His kingdom wherever He sends me. At times, we do kingdom audits, reflecting on how faithfully we have cared for what belongs to each other. In hindsight, He has proven to be a masterful steward of my dreams, bringing them to life one after another. Each day, I bear more fruit for Him, grow in ambition for Heaven's kingdom, and help others know Him deeply.

Luke 9:23

ROYAL NAVY

The Captain feasted each night with his crew, inviting every rank to the table, bonding with laughter and full hearts. The crew learned to savor each other's presence and gained self-control, no longer ruled by endless consumption. They knew there was always enough. They felt like royalty, and they wanted to treat one another as such. This spirit of generosity spilled over, and they welcomed everyone they met as if they were already kings. It was as if the ragtag pirates of the ***Golden Tide*** *were being transformed into a Royal Navy. When a new man joined, the first question was always,* ***How can we make him feel like a king?*** *Most pirates came from hardship, drawn into lives of taking and harming in search of peace, yet newcomers soon felt like royalty after being so warmly welcomed by the strong, content sailors.*

Hospitality is at the core of the kingdom, and the size of a house or a person's expertise is no barrier. My Florida apartment was a tiny studio where I often hosted dinners and communion for groups of people who were happy to be there. It's about the host treating everyone like royalty and creating a space where they feel safe to be their authentic selves. Sharing a meal is powerful because it can build more real connection in one evening than a whole year of sitting invisibly in the same pew every Sunday. I like to think that if I were hosting Jesus for dinner tonight, I would ask who to invite, what to serve, and how He would treat the guests. The truth is, because the Holy Spirit lives in me, when I walk in obedience to God, those I speak with are, in a way, encountering Jesus through me. He is there in how I host, and the guests get to interact with Him while feasting. People can't help but be transformed when treated like royalty, as Jesus does. Whatever each person's gift is, whether it is hospitality, healing, wisdom, or miracles, it should be shared freely with the world that truly needs it.

Romans 8:16-17

L.O.V.E

Peg Leg pulled the Captain aside, saying that he had never known such peace aboard a ship. For the first time in his weary life, Peg Leg felt like a true passenger, no longer weighed down by constant fear. The reason was clear: the Captain's choice to share his wealth freely with the crew. Every sailor knew he had a rightful share of the treasure, and that knit them together as brothers. Through the Captain's loving generosity, the band of rogues became a loyal family, and Peg Leg poured his soul into his work, sailing now for the joy of the journey.

A video of a robot performing surgery on a grape went viral during my junior year of college, showcasing robotic arms remotely controlled by a surgeon through joysticks and a viewfinder. With astonishing precision, the surgeon guided the robot to peel back a diamond-shaped section of grape skin and suture it neatly back into place, delicate work that highlighted the potential of this technology. Yet without the surgeon, the arms would have been useless, for they only brought healing by responding faithfully to his every command. Their brilliance lay in perfect synchronicity with the doctor's motions, which is why the video captured the world's imagination. In the same way, God works through Christians to bring life and healing to this world, guiding His people as the true physician while they act as His instruments. If the robot arms had merely repeated the same motions from one surgery to another, they could have caused harm through misguided guesswork, for every body is unique, and in the same way every soul requires its own care to feel loved. God alone knows the perfect movements, since He created them. From my experience, the most successful way to participate in this healing is to live attuned and responsive, by following the acronym **L.O.V.E.**: **L.**istening and **O.**beying the **V.**oice of **E.**lohim. When believers allow God's love to flow through them, every life they touch begins to find peace, just as the crew found peace once the Captain let his wealth flow to everyone.

John 15:12

Tending Soil

The Captain's heart warmed as he reflected on Peg Leg's words. He thought back to his first week, lost in a windless sea, questioning whether he was a leader at all. The memory sparked a vision of his father tending his fields in England, his strong yet gentle hands working the soil with care. His father never forced the grain to grow by shouting or demanding. Instead, he recognized what each seed was meant to become and provided what it needed: sunlight, water, and an occasional pruning, so it could flourish in its own time. The Captain smiled, realizing that leading a pirate crew was not so different. A good Captain, like a good farmer, does not control through pressure but nurtures with generosity, guidance, and gentle correction. He marveled at how this approach, offering his crew what they truly needed, had begun to transform them day by day. Force only bred exasperation, but true care inspired loyalty and growth.

When getting to know people through *"pirate feasts"* at home, all sorts of unique individuals show up, and I've noticed that friction naturally arises as intimacy deepens. There is no need to fear hosting people who are different or hard to relate to. Shepherding well means boldly using the L.O.V.E. acronym to love others, no matter how unrelatable their circumstances may seem. When I hear God's voice and speak what He leads me to say to someone, that is the essence of prophecy. It really is that simple. Honestly sharing the words God directs provides the perfect balance of sunlight, rain, pruning, or even silence needed for everyone to bear maximum fruit. It is amazing to see God's character emerge through this practice, revealing His heart to correct those who are strong and close to Him while showing mercy and healing to those who are hurt, needy, or distant. Love is closely tied to attention, so giving God and others full focus means putting away phones and other distractions during gatherings. Living things grow, and in the safe soil of a godly home, people cannot help but flourish.

1 Corinthians 3:6-7

CURIOUS CATCH

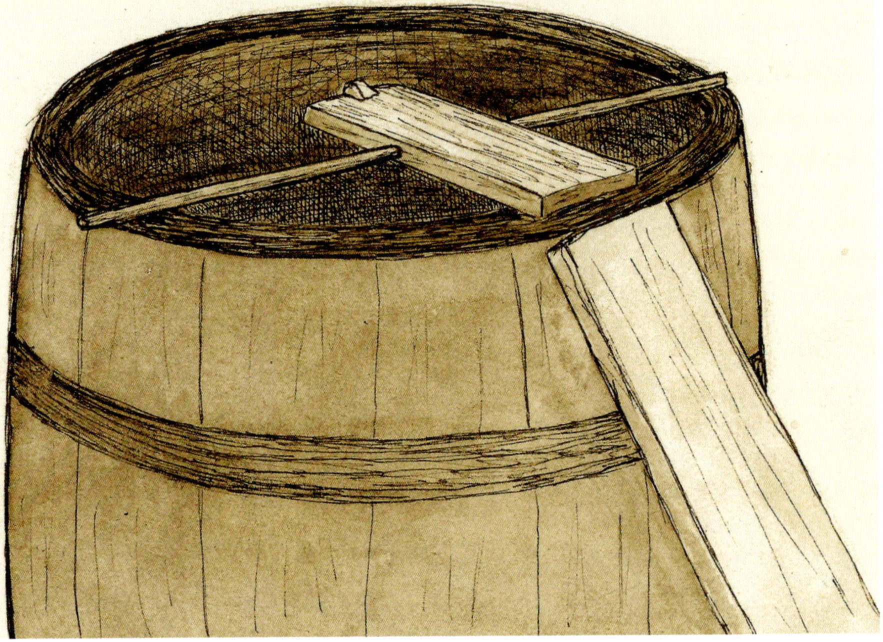

With four days left before reaching Port Royal, a trio of pet monkeys escaped from their cage below deck and were wreaking havoc across the ship, stealing food, scattering supplies, and climbing the rigging, mocking the crew from above. So the pirates turned to trapping techniques they'd learned in Aruba. The natives taught that trapping animals wasn't just about baited cages, but about understanding the animal's world. It was like solving a complex puzzle that required patience and careful observation. The pirates studied the monkeys; where they played, what they avoided, what tempted them, where they felt safe at different times of day, what senses they relied on most, and even which animals they trusted or feared. Luring them in seemed impossible at first, but they persevered. Only by answering these questions could they set traps that the monkeys would walk into by choice. Through persistence, they recaptured their monkeys without harm.

Jesus built friendships over meals rather than chasing quick conversions. He led with curiosity, asking nearly 300 recorded questions that invited dialogue and empathy. Like studying a monkey's habits to guide it willingly, His questions drew seekers toward God freely, not by force but by safety and trust. While hosting at home, here are 10 questions to help get to know people with curiosity at *"pirate feasts."* A funny question to start with: *What are the pirates saying on the decks of your mind? What gets you fired up in life? What's something you love talking about but don't often get to share? What's God been up to in your life in the past week? What's a miracle you'd like to see God do? Is there anything you need right now? How can I be a better friend to you? What's a question you wish people asked you more often? If God were sitting right here with us, what would you tell Him?* If someone shares honest pains or fears, see if they're open to praying and listening for the Holy Spirit's perspective by saying, *"Would you like to ask God now to share His thoughts on your situation?"*

Acts 2:44-45

SPECIAL FORCES

The Caribbean was a fierce and unforgiving place. With treacherous pirates lurking around coves, attacking both merchant ships and rival crews, most travelers stayed sharp, always ready for trouble. Skirmishes weren't a matter of if, but when, which is why the Captain made sure his crew kept their fighting skills sharp as a cutlass. They practiced manning the cannons, wrestling on the deck, and crossing blades in swordplay, building their strength so there'd be no chance of losing if an enemy ship attacked. Training together, they became more than a crew; they became a tight-knit band of brothers who could predict each other's moves like the back of their own hand. It was like being part of a pirate navy's finest, hand-picked by the Captain for their courage and cunning. The more they trained, the more they trusted one another, knowing full well that victory at sea came not from a single pirate's skill, but from the power of the crew as one. No matter how skilled, a lone sailor would stand no chance against an enemy ship. Together, though, they were unstoppable.

I like to think of myself as part of Heaven's special forces. Two key questions arise. First, how much time should I spend training with other Christians versus time spent in battle against demonic forces while saving lost souls? Many churches rush people into spiritual battles with shallow teaching and loose connections, leading to casualties of faith. But Jesus spent years forging a close-knit band of 12 before sending them out, showing that true strength is built through time, trust, and shared purpose. Second, how could I possibly fight against the devil on my own? I've realized I can't confront the enemy by myself. However gifted I might be, I need mates who know God deeply to challenge, strengthen, and stand with me when the fight is fiercest. True spiritual warfare demands a unified crew forged through prayer, obedience, and horizontal edification. Without that, I'd be as reckless as a single sailor charging a hostile ship. But with them, I'm prepared for any storm the enemy brings.

Ecclesiastes 4:12

CAST SHEEP

The great thing about the crew becoming a tight-knit unit was how, when one stumbled or faced hard times, the others were quick to help him up. Every man needed support now and then, whether it was a shoulder to lean on, someone to talk to, or simply a bit of time to rest. It reminded the Captain of the sheep his childhood neighbor kept. They would often fall onto their backs, becoming what was called a cast sheep. They might topple from the weight of their thick wool, get stuck after sleeping in a ditch, or collapse under a heavy rain-soaked coat. They were not the cleverest creatures, and without the shepherd to set them right, they could die in the heat within a few hours. Pirates also could fall under the weight of life's burdens, but the difference was that they always had their mates nearby to lift them up again.

There were many times while writing this book when I felt hopeless, but my friends helped me see the truth and find my footing again. I often got discouraged by my dyslexia and slow progress, wanting to quit. Before adapting the parables into the pirate meta-narrative, I worried about how to market the book in relatable ways. Halfway through the illustrations, my illustrator's dad had a heart attack, and his aunt passed away in the same week, delaying us for multiple weeks and making me fear we wouldn't finish. Then God led me to self-publish, which felt extremely risky, as I had open doors with major publishers. Through it all, my crew reminded me that God is faithful to complete what He begins, that this book was already finished in heaven, and I was just uncovering it. Living in close community with regular home dinners lets me share burdens in ways that aren't practical in a large church service. Some of my rhythms include meals with a close friend and mentor, two discipleship groups, weekday phone calls with five close friends, and monthly Shabbat dinners, all of which help me stay on track wherever God sends me.

Ecclesiastes 4:9-10

FAT BOY

The hot Caribbean spring sun brought the Captain back to rough boyhood afternoons on the village green. The local lads played a fierce sort of ball game with only a few rules, a heavy leather ball, and a mob of shouting boys chasing and shoving through mud and grass. He remembered them jeering at him: ***"Oi, if you don't want to stay fat and friendless, come play with us!"*** *More of a dare than an invitation. Driven by fear and a need to belong, he charged in. Now, standing on the deck as Captain, he was glad he didn't recruit his crew that way. He didn't bark,* ***"You look poor and lost, want to fix that with us?"*** *Instead, he asked,* ***"Do you want to get wealthy with me?"*** *and waited.*

Jesus never held up hellfire and brimstone signs demanding *"convert or burn,"* nor did He deliver slick sales pitches for quick conversions. Instead, He announced that the Kingdom of Heaven was at hand; God's reign breaking into the world. And He embodied this good news through friendship, hospitality, and care for sinners. Evangelism isn't about manipulation, confrontation, or making people feel judged with questions like, *"Do you know where you're going after you die?"* Such tactics often create defensiveness, damage relationships, and push people away rather than draw them in. I used to fear that moving away from traditional corporate church evangelism, with its big buildings, budgets, and altar calls, would leave nothing for people to discover and cause the whole church to collapse. It seemed that if the church focused inward on loving one another in small, close-knit communities, there would be less fruit for the kingdom. But I discovered the opposite. As believers grow healthy together, meeting each other's needs, sharing meals, and genuinely enjoying life by tasting heaven on earth, those around them take notice. The world sees the joy, strength, and unmistakable light of people overflowing with God's presence. It sparks curiosity and a longing, naturally drawing people in and building trust so they can explore God at their own pace, without pressure or force.

John 13:35

SCRIMMAGE

The Captain didn't enjoy the rugged games on the village green. They turned ugly fast, with shouting, shoving, and cheap shots in the mud. The jeers from the other lads and the pressure to prove himself only made it worse. His mind would race, and he'd blunder, getting knocked down harder by boys eager to pummel the small kid. But Sundays were different. His best friend, an older classmate and neighbor, would pull him aside to practice alone. They'd work on throwing the ball just right or timing clever runs through the grass. Without the external pressure, the game slowed down. Over weeks of these quiet scrimmages, he found himself laughing, trying new moves, and realizing that he could read the chaos and play better. Soon, in real games, he started slipping past defenders, enjoying himself, and shocking everyone.

I used to think that having full control of my own life would be the ultimate freedom, but it turned out to be painfully hard. I had to take full blame for every mistake, and life felt like a relentless game of survival with everything to lose and the stakes impossibly high. But who doesn't want to join a fun scrimmage of pickup of any sport where everyone is laughing, encouraging each other, and not risking their life for the next point? When I finally gave my life to God and started getting to know Christians, I noticed that some of the godliest people I met are also the funniest. Life is so much more fun and less serious when I realized I no longer had to fear anything. Being a Christian feels a lot like playing in a scrimmage where the burden of winning is lifted from my shoulders because the outcome is already assured. Jesus overcame death itself, leaving no reason to fear. I've learned that if life with God doesn't feel enjoyable or filled with His peace, then something essential is missing, and it's time to reevaluate, because it is only God who gives humans the ability to enjoy anything on earth, whether in abundance or in need.

Ecclesiastes 5:19-20

Winning Strategy

During the rough games, the Captain learned a surprising lesson: go where no one else was. When he first joined in, fear ruled his every move. He stuck close to the mass of boys, afraid of fumbling the ball or being trampled in the mud. But as he kept playing, something clicked. He noticed that when everyone crowded together, the ball got lost, and no one could advance. So he tried doing the opposite. Instead of staying packed in with the others, he ran into open patches of grass. At first, it felt wrong and left him exposed, but soon he saw that it gave him an edge. By stepping away from the chaos, he made space for the ball to find him. In the wild scramble of the game, space made all the difference, but stepping into it required courage.

Following others' callings in Christianity once felt safe, but to not clog the field, it's essential to draw close to God as my coach and listen for His voice so I know where to run to win. God called me to create an entrepreneurial community. It felt scary to step into that open space, but His plans see beyond what I imagined. That's how I created **Wonser Park LLC** (WonserPark.com), *a family of innovators building at God's speed*. The vision is to build a physical space like Edison's innovation lab but grounded in faith, bringing God's presence into the marketplace. This dream is fueled by a patronage model to cultivate the gifts of young people within a business setting while discipling them as children of the King, rather than as merchants of this world. I envision a work culture where each team member learns to recognize God's voice and is empowered to obey it without hesitation, trusting that the One who knows the future leads far better than any human hierarchy. I envision a facility on 60+ acres, serving the city with trails, bikes, food for sale, live concerts, retreats, and rugged camping on-site to unite people enjoying God's creation. I never imagined my first invention would be a book, but in His wisdom, God led me to make it the first innovative product from this collaborative community, setting a clear foundation that points back to Him.

Joshua 1:7

P.I.R.A.T.E.

*As **Golden Tide** docked in Port Royal, the Captain felt nostalgic, intending to invite old friends to join the fleet. Yet the town had changed, or perhaps he had. After months among a crew who had grown more disciplined and self-controlled, the Captain was stunned by the beastly state of the locals. Old companions turned cold, pushing him away out of jealousy when they saw how prosperous his crew had become. Many scoffed at the invitation, insisting their next raid would bring fortune. Most weren't humble enough to receive unearned blessings, nor desperate enough to admit they weren't wealthy. And not all who did join the crew had pure motives. Some hearts were riddled with greed, secretly aiming to divide the crew and steal when the time felt right. The Captain, discerning their intent, quickly cast them out, knowing such poison would sink the ship from within.*

Early in my walk with God, I grew close to friends who were struggling in their faith. We got along well, but over time, they headed down destructive paths distant from the Father, and I felt myself being pulled down too. I thought I could stay strong and help them, but because they held a deep place in my heart, their choices affected me more than I expected. God prompted me to speak up, and I warned them several times. When they didn't listen, I knew I had to step away. It was heartbreaking, but it protected my heart from destruction. Like a pirate Captain who talks with lost pirates on land but must return to lead his own crew, I realized I needed to choose my closest companions carefully. When choosing comrades, I've learned to look for the marks of a true pirate. Someone whose heart is good soil and whose life bears Kingdom fruit. To help me discern this, I use a simple **P.I.R.A.T.E.** acronym: **P**ractice Curiosity, **I**nspire Generosity, **R**esolve Conflict, **A**ccept Responsibility, **T**alk Honestly, and **E**xpress Emotions. These traits reveal whether a person is ready to sail with integrity and unity, or whether they'll pull the crew off course.

Proverbs 13:20

ISLAND RATIONS

Port Royal was becoming less comfortable for the Captain. In pubs, pirates jeered and spread false tales, mocking him as a foolish leader who forgot vital supplies at every island his ship visited. What they did not know, or chose to ignore, was the truth. Long ago, the Captain weathered violent hurricane winds, certain he and the crew would be shipwrecked and starve on some remote shore. That storm changed him. From then on, whenever his ship visited an island, he left behind extra wheat and rigging in public caches, hoping to give future shipwrecked sailors a fighting chance. But now, those selfless actions had been twisted into false rumors. Pirates who once shared his table suddenly painted him as an outsider, trying to push him out to protect their fragile pride. Even so, the Captain stood firm, knowing his heart was clear and his hands had only sown kindness into the soil of the sea.

A friend of mine in Nashville heard God call him to build a massive addition to his house, a large open space with 20-foot ceilings that could seat about 150 people for kingdom gatherings. He lived in a nice neighborhood, but he trusted God and started construction anyway, carefully matching the new space to his existing home design so it looked excellent. He had no idea what God would use it for. I call that bold faith. As construction started, persecution arose. Neighbors grew furious, judging him from a distance as selfish and gaudy without asking intentions. They spread rumors that his project would devalue homes, hurting the neighborhood, fighting permits, and straining relationships. But God told him to keep building. His tenacity to obey reminded me of the woman who poured expensive perfume on Jesus' feet, unconcerned with others' judgments over her extravagant devotion. Some called it wasteful, squandering a year's salary, but God saw it as an act worthy of Heaven's hall of fame. My friend's new space will be finished in a couple of months, and he's still waiting to see what God has planned for it.

John 12:1-8

PLAY THE SONG

After days of enduring scorn from the town, the crew returned to their ship one evening, feeling weary and discouraged. But as they gathered for their nightly feast, the Captain stood and lifted their spirits with a simple call. He said there was no reason to waste breath trying to explain how good this crew was; the city must feel it for themselves. That night, the crew would sing with such joy that the wind would carry their melodies all the way to Tortuga, so the entire Caribbean would know the spirit of the ***Golden Tide.*** *At his word, the crew grabbed every fiddle, pennywhistle, drum, accordion, and tambourine they could find. Standing shoulder to shoulder on the deck, they sang with hearts wide open, their voices ringing out into the harbor. The shanties soared above the waves and through the streets, and there was not a soul in Port Royal who could ignore it. That night became a historic memory, the most joyful sound the city had ever known and would ever know, as if heaven itself had visited the harbor and sung through the crew of the* ***Golden Tide.***

Now that I've found true connection with God, I want the song of my life to play for the world to hear. That means walking in divine flow, Listening and Obeying the Voice of Elohim, and building up fellow Christians through regular gatherings like pirate feasts in homes. The world is starving to hear this beautiful song that shows the Kingdom of Heaven is here and now. I pray that the melody of my life is so compelling that others can't get it out of their heads, and that every room I enter carries the lingering fragrance of God's presence. It is time to help restore the world, to create a society where people are thoughtful and trustworthy, and where money is no longer the ultimate goal. I pray for a world where every orphan has a home, every widow is cared for, the poor are made rich, and every stranger finds a place to belong. Let Heaven invade!

James 1:27

FOOL'S GOLD

The Captain woke the next morning, planning to trade the three barrels of fine salt they had received as gifts in Aruba. Salt production was scarce near Port Royal, and the barrels altogether could sell for three gold coins. As he transported the barrels through town toward Merchant's Alley, pirates along the road glared with silent fury. The joyful singing from the ***Golden Tide*** *the night before had pushed them over the edge. When he reached the merchant, the man received the salt eagerly and, without argument, handed over three gold coins. But the moment the Captain felt them in his palm, he knew the truth. Years of handling his own gold treasure had taught him well; these were fakes. The merchant was trying to cheat him. The Captain dropped the coins to the ground in disgust, hoisted his barrels back onto the cart, and turned toward the harbor. Port Royal, a city that once felt alive with promise, was rotten with lying, cheating, and stealing. He decided to leave and set sail to venture westward.*

Lives are complicated, and it can be hard to tell at first glance who is truly close to God and who is pretending. Many things can cloud judgment: charisma, age, similarity, intellectualism, status, emotional expression, and even acts of service. Words alone can be deceptive; declaring faith or denomination can be as shallow as a sailor donning another crew's flag colors to avoid conflict. The real question is whether God knows them intimately. Many know about the King of England, but only those he knows personally are invited to his wedding feast. It takes patient observation to see if God is in their heart. I've found the best way to recognize this fruit is by spending time with God's Spirit and His church, learning what tangible kingdom fruit looks like lived out. True spiritual fruit grows naturally, not through forced effort. The more I treasure God's presence and the fellowship of His people, the better I become at recognizing genuine spiritual fruit in others and discerning spiritual counterfeits from a mile away.

Matthew 7:23

CONSPIRACY

Bitter whispers filled taverns as the ***Golden Tide*** *left Port Royal. Enraged by their friction with the Captain and threatened by his growing crew, jealous pirates wove lies. They claimed he'd never found treasure, only lured sailors with promises of gold, robbed them at sea, and tossed bodies overboard. Fueled by envy and fear, they convinced themselves this twisted tale explained his success. The lie spread like wildfire, hardening into belief. Determined to punish the Captain for crimes he never committed, they cobbled together a vicious crew of drifters, outcasts, and killers bent on revenge. With sails raised and fury in their hearts, the rogue ship set out, vowing to end the legend of the* ***Golden Tide****.*

I've heard pastors say that Americans should be thankful to live in a country without persecution, but the truth is, the enemy mainly targets those actively advancing God's kingdom. Spiritual warfare is very real for those merging heaven and earth. The closer I've drawn to God, the more evident, and sometimes physically dangerous, the opposition has become. My friend Ben has survived many random knife and gun attacks. A mentor of mine received unmarked boxes multiple times filled with pornography delivered to his doorstep with his name on them that he didn't order, causing tension in his marriage until they recognized it as spiritual warfare. I've seen the enemy attack relationships in my own life, too. After meeting Randy, I spent months believing wild accusations about him, that he'd led the January 6th Capitol attacks, was banned from all colleges, and was a satan worshipper. But when I finally met with him again, I found one of the most loving, God-fearing men I'd ever known. The enemy had nearly succeeded in ruining a powerful friendship. These kinds of attacks have reminded me to stay armored up and spiritually alert. I'm not trying to stir fear, but I do wish someone had warned me sooner that the more I push back the darkness, the more resistance I'll face, because I become a threat to the enemy. And yet, God's protection shows up ever more.

Ephesians 6:12

DECISIVE VICTORY

*Catching up to the **Golden Tide**, the rogue ship flew red flags, signaling no mercy and certain death if they resisted. The Captain's heart ached at their hardened hearts, knowing blood would be spilled. His crew took battle stations with weapons ready. The pirates on the rogue ship howled in rage, firing cannons too far to hit, using sound and smoke to strike fear. Yet the **Golden Tide's** calm crew stood firm, knowing this would be a decisive victory. They had trained relentlessly and would fight for their lives, their brothers, and the treasure they possessed. When the enemy ship came within range, the Captain gave the order. Cannons thundered, ripping into the ship's hull. The blast ignited powder stores, triggering an explosion that tore the vessel in two. Within minutes, the rogue ship sank.*

A godly inventor friend partnered with another self-proclaiming Christian to bring his divinely inspired product to market. They spent months preparing for a major acquisition meeting. Days before, God assured my friend He would protect him from schemes formed against him, a cryptic promise at the time. On the day of the meeting, he arrived alone and received devastating news: his partner and the partner's wife had died in a car accident on the way. As he processed the shock, the company shared additional painful news. His partner had secretly planned to cut him out of the deal and keep the money. It was sobering, but my friend recognized God's protection from a wolf in sheep's clothing. It showed how closely God watches over those walking in obedience to Him. While Christians never desire harm for anyone, confidence rests in God's ability to handle opposition as He sees fit. These moments grieve His heart, yet He would rather protect the flock than risk losing them. He is gracious toward those who genuinely seek Him and toward the lost who do not yet know Him, but Scripture and experience show He resists those who knowingly work against His purposes. God is kind and gracious, yet just, fiercely defending His children as they walk in His will.

Isaiah 54:17

SUNKEN CITY
1692

*As the **Golden Tide** crew roared in victory, sharing celebratory hugs, the Captain stood on the quarterdeck, gazing in deep thought over the sunken ship. He soon gathered the men and unexpectedly announced that they would return to Port Royal. He explained that those pirates clearly didn't understand their message of peace and invitation to join, so they must return to share the truth again. So they sailed back, but when they reached the coast late one afternoon, confusion turned to horror. The city was gone. The entire peninsula had vanished in some catastrophe of nature and was swallowed by the sea. Floating wreckage marked where the bustling port once stood, and it became clear that a massive earthquake must have struck, drowning the city alive. As they drew closer, they saw thousands of lifeless bodies drifting in the water, a graveyard of those who had once mocked them. The Captain's heart broke. Among the wreckage, a few dozen survivors clung to debris in shark-infested waters, screaming for help. With no hesitation, the crew pulled them aboard. Grateful and desperate, the survivors joined the crew, knowing it was life or death.*

Jesus makes His disciples into fishers of men, which at first sounds strange because it brings to mind an image of men in the water where they don't belong. Yet the truth is that most people are spiritually drowning, and it is the church's mission to rescue them onto solid ground so they can live a full life. In a mysterious act of grace, God chooses to partner with imperfect people like me to help save the world, calling His children to be known by love rather than symbols. Jesus never forced anyone to follow. He moved on when people refused to listen, like a captain who doesn't linger among those loyal to enemy fleets but leads those willing to follow His voice. God's good news invites all to come aboard the ship that brings true wealth. My role is to share hope, peace, and salvation, offering others the chance to experience the fullness of God's presence, starting now.

Matthew 4:19

WINSHIP

Amidst the wreckage of shattered hulls and sunken dreams, one ship stood untouched, a massive, gleaming vessel that looked freshly captured, oddly absent during their last port visit. Curious how it survived the earthquake when all others were wrecked or washed ashore, the crew of the ***Golden Tide*** *pulled alongside and called out across the silent decks. No one answered. As Peg Leg boarded and searched the ship, it became clear no soul remained to claim it. He reappeared on the main deck with a grin, declaring they had just won the ship lottery. With a hearty laugh, the Captain claimed it as the first official addition to their growing fleet and appointed Peg Leg as its Captain. Swelling with pride, Peg Leg gathered his mates, took the helm, and named his new vessel the* ***Winship.*** *With that, the two captains, bound by honor and now a fleet, looked across the harbor at one another marveling in quiet wonder. The Captain's long-held dream of starting a fleet had finally taken shape, no longer a distant hope but a reality at hand, and the crew felt their strength had already more than doubled.*

The Latin word for priest is synonymous with bridge, capturing God's call for His people to be a Kingdom of priests, each person anointed as a bridge for God to cross and bring heaven into this broken world. Countless lost souls wait in a foreign land, needing someone to build that bridge to rescue them. When the church links arms to introduce people to God, it becomes an unstoppable force. God promises to provide everything His children need for the mission He has given them, whether transportation, finances, housing, or relationships. This is the year of the pirate, and God's fleet is growing stronger than ever! God is training up small crews in homes to burst forth into fleets to spread true wealth over cities, states, countries, and, soon enough, the entire world.

1 Peter 2:9

FOREIGN COINS

Exploring the new ship felt like Christmas to Peg Leg. The vessel was strong and equally as large as the **Golden Tide**. *As they searched its decks, they discovered it had once been a Spanish pirate ship, recently captured and brought into port just before the earthquake. To their amazement, the warship's supplies were still fully intact. The biggest surprise came when Peg Leg uncovered a locked chest in the captain's quarters. He broke it open, hoping to find a trove of gold. But instead, it was filled with maravedís, Spanish copper coins that were worthless outside of Spain. They were better off melted into tools or traded for scraps. Though disappointed, Peg Leg laughed at the irony. For now, the Captain's existing stockpile of gold would be the only currency usable in these parts of the world. Luckily, there was still enough gold left in his chest to suffice for the rest of their lives.*

I imagine sitting in heaven, admiring the design of a $100 bill, remembering how valuable it once seemed under another government, yet realizing it is now just worthless paper in heaven's economy. From an eternal perspective, worldly wealth has little value because it cannot bring lasting fulfillment in life and loses all worth at death. I've found that having less money can actually be a gift, helping me sense when God wants me to begin or end something. He provides resources when He wants doors to open and withholds them when it is time to close them. It is strangely comforting to live in that foggy place of need. My friends and I practice something called *"Treasure Checks,"* where we reflect on the past week to find golden moments of genuine connection with God. Remembering these treasures keeps us focused on intimacy with Him and less distracted by the world's frivolous pleasures and stressors. Just as it would be concerning if a husband had nothing positive to say about his wife's recent interactions, it is also a warning sign if a follower of Jesus cannot recall any treasured moments with Him in that time.

Matthew 6:19-21

CAVE RESCUE

Peg Leg suddenly remembered the cave where the priest had once tended to his injured leg. He knew if anyone had survived the quake, they might have taken shelter there. Without delay, both crews hiked inland to rescue any who remained. Deep inside the cave, after winding through tunnels, they discovered a huddled group of terrified survivors shielding their eyes from the bright torches. They had lost everything and now sat shivering in the damp darkness, hungry and disoriented. They had tried finding the way out but had only wandered deeper into the maze. When the pirates offered rescue and space aboard their new ship, many doubted. Some cried, ***"You're lying. You just want to rob us."*** *Others whispered,* ***"I don't deserve to be saved. I abandoned my mates."*** *But the crew replied that they, too, were once cowards, and still they were chosen. Most stayed behind, but two men rose and followed, stepping into the narrow path that led to light and a new life among Peg Leg's crew.*

Any spelunker knows the magical feeling of leaving a cave and feeling the soft, warm touch of sunlight. How wonderful it is to bask in spiritual light all day, relaxing in God's presence, and be with Him. I was designed to live in the light of God's presence. But God's voice constantly reminds me never to forget what it felt like when I was stuck in the cave, shivering, lonely, anxious, hurting myself trying to find a way out. God has anointed His followers to go back into that dark cave to find other lost children of the King and show them the way out. Wouldn't they love to feel the sunlight as much as I did? The Spirit provides the perfect light to guide me as I search for others in need. My mission is to put on my headlamp, break down the gates of hellish caves to let heaven invade, and offer the lost the true way out into the life-giving light of God. So here I go, to somewhere dangerous, to bring back something precious.

Isiah 61:1

SHAKESPEARE

Upon exiting the cave, the Captain was puzzled by the many who refused rescue, both there and earlier in Port Royal. The truth had been freely offered, yet some simply couldn't believe it was that simple. His mind wandered back to childhood in Shaftesbury and a rare family trip to London to see ***The Merry Wives of Windsor*** *performed live. He loved it so much he eagerly described it to classmates back home, only to be mocked for liking something they thought was girlish and silly. It hurt, but he realized even then their ridicule came from ignorance. None of them had seen Shakespeare performed, so their words held no real weight. They probably would have loved it too if they'd experienced it themselves. The same was true now. The* ***Golden Tide*** *was an honest crew working to bless the world with their treasure, and anyone claiming otherwise was simply blind to the truth. If people refused to join, that burden was no longer his to carry.*

When the movie *Dune* was released in 2021, it sparked conversations everywhere. As a sci-fi fan who hadn't read the books, I went in with high hopes but left frustrated, convinced it was either a terrible film or too complex for me to understand. I shared my disappointment widely, criticizing its slow plot and confusing storytelling. Months later, I brought it up with my illustrator, Stephen, a true movie buff. To my surprise, he called *Dune* one of the best films he'd ever seen and offered to rewatch it with me, pausing to explain its depth in context. That experience changed my perspective and reminded me of my relationship with God. Just because someone criticizes God doesn't mean I should doubt His goodness if I've truly experienced it. Like Stephen, confident in his love for *Dune*, I'm called to patiently share my encounters with God's love and truth. My role is to be a friend who offers understanding rather than forcing belief, trusting that over time others might come to see the God I see, just as I eventually understood and loved *Dune*.

Luke 8:17

LIVE FOREVER

*The Captain and Peg Leg discussed where they should sail next, with a second ship and a free schedule. Suddenly, the man they had rescued from the skiff in the middle of the ocean a while back, shouted with confidence, "**North!**" He spoke of an ancient legend, a Fountain of Youth hidden farther north near a city called St. Augustine. He claimed that if they found it, the entire crew might live forever. The offer sounded absurd, but there was something in the man's voice that stirred their sense of wonder. Intrigued, the Captain and Peg Leg agreed. As they sailed north, the Captain leaned against the railing, imagining living forever. What would he do with endless time? Could he explore every land and culture on the map? The idea felt like a dream, wild and impossible, yet full of promise.*

What would I do if I never died and lived forever on this earth? What feeling arises immediately after imagining that? What would I change about my lifestyle? How would I treat people differently? Would I continue working the same job? Would I go to Sunday church services? Would I move to a new town? Would I be content with my current life with God forever here? Jesus focused His message on reviving this world and uniting heaven and earth. The Bible rarely even talks about the afterlife. While there definitely is life beyond this one, Jesus urges the Church to focus on today's challenges instead of solely worrying about the afterlife. The Kingdom of Heaven is already here, calling me to do the Father's will today and trust Him deeply. He's a good Father in this life and the next. I don't need to fear the end of the world, since His perfect love casts out fear. I get to enjoy the treasure of knowing Him on earth since heaven begins now. I choose to live as if He returns tomorrow, while managing my life carefully as if He may never return in my lifetime.

John 4:14

FIND YOUR TREASURE

Sailing north for the **Fountain of Youth***, the Captain pondered what would change if he lived forever. He remembered the day he unearthed the buried treasure chest in Florida. That unexpected gift had transformed every corner of his life. He never knew who had left it there or why, but the generosity of that unseen giver marked him forever as treasure he did not earn or deserve. And so, he made a vow to live out the name of his ship by becoming a true tide of gold across the world. Since then, he began hiding gold coins wherever he traveled, wanting to spark the same wonder and hope he once felt. Word spread of a pirate who gave rather than took, hiding wealth throughout the world to attract all the landlocked people to overcome their fears, brave the seas, and find their treasure. And legend has it, to this day, his coins are still out there, waiting to be found by those bold enough to search.*

All I want now is to share the wealth of spiritual truths in this book with other curious faith seekers. To make it fun, I'm launching a large-scale treasure hunt that everyone can join. For every ten books sold, I'll hide a special brass coin somewhere around the US. These coins will match the collector's coin visualized in this parable, and anyone who finds one can redeem it for a free copy of the book. I'll share clues on social media at **@pirateparables** to help people find them, encouraging folks to put down their phones and explore the real world to discover their treasure. A total of 1,000 brass coins will be hidden, and as a grand finale, once they're all placed, I'll announce that one has been secretly swapped for a genuine gold coin, so the hunt will continue. It's a wonderful adventure to invite curious friends who are searching for spiritual truth to join the hunt, strengthen bonds of friendship, and experience the goodness of God together. For details, visit **www.pirateparables.com**. Bon voyage, fellow pirate! Find your treasure!

Jeremiah 29:13

CONCLUSION

If you've ever felt like **a lost pirate** chasing **hollow victories**, take heart. God invites you to lay down your **cards** and let Him win your trust. In His presence you'll find healing, strength to conquer the **giants ahead**, and the greatest treasure of all: His voice. Don't stay **landlocked**. **Find your treasure**! The real gold is not simply knowing about God but knowing Him in a living, conversational relationship. Hearing His voice unlocks everything else: He reveals your true identity and calling, uncovers your giftings, and leads you to the people He longs for you to love. He guides your steps in the Father's will daily, teaches you how to gather as Christ's body, and shows you the problems He designed you to solve.

His voice, as the captain of your vessel, transforms you into a **golden tide** that brightens the dark world, like **moonlight** reflecting His face the more you gaze at Him. Your surrender becomes the **canvas** for His masterpiece. **Celebrate with your mates** so that life does not shrink into **mass production**. **Stop & help** your crew so that your ship stays **sturdy** and link arms with true **P.I.R.A.T.E.**s who would row **160 miles** alongside you to find the treasure. Being part of God's **royal navy** of **L.O.V.E.** is the **winning strategy** of life, so **play the song** for all to hear. **Conspiracies** fall flat, **fearmongers** fade, and **decisive victories** follow.

Don't sit in jealousy of the treasure in my life; it isn't because I'm more special than you. The same treasure is yours to discover and keep. Our journeys won't be carbon copies. What we WILL have in common is always diving deeper in knowing God. Step onto the gangplank of Scripture, board His ship, and embrace the adventure of partnering with His presence to restore the earth. Anyone hungry enough to seek the treasure of His voice will find it. Do not fear. Sail off into The Mystery. Your life will never be the same.

Romans 15:13

Thank you so much for taking the time to read *Pirate Parables*. I'd truly love to hear from you, so if you'd like to share how this book has impacted you or have any questions, feel free to email me directly at **parker@pirateparables.com**. If you're like me and enjoy more tangible connection via handwritten letters or thoughtful packages, you're always welcome to send them to:

4884 Port Royal Rd Ste 120 #160, Spring Hill, TN 37174

Each parable is packed with rich meaning that many readers have found worth revisiting slowly, savoring the wisdom in every story. Children especially enjoy hearing the pirate adventures read aloud without the testimonies while exploring the beautiful illustrations that bring the journey to life. It has amazed me to see God use this book to revive hearts in our chaotic religious and political climate, spreading whispers of another world and offering a backdoor entrance into His Kingdom.

This book would not have been possible without the invaluable teachings of **Marty Solomon**, **Tom Wadsworth**, and **Jamie Winship**. I am also deeply grateful to the generous donors who made this project possible: Diane and Rick Jones, Mac Bloodworth, Josey and Josh Gonzalez, Johan Glidden, Alan Lennon, Terence Halonie, Ben Watson, Brian Clark, Kylee Robin, Margaret Wonser, Luke Marchesani, Gregory Skye, Tim Kelly, Wayne Garvey, Blake Ruby, Evan Greathouse, Jeff and Nancy Wonser, and Dakota Crespo.

My prayer is that *Pirate Parables* has drawn you closer to Jesus. May you enjoy the rich life of a spiritual pirate under the command of our Good Captain. I hope we meet in this life, and if not, I look forward to seeing you in the next.

Stay bold, **Parker Wonser**